THE ORACLES
Beginnings: Earth and Air

by Katherine Madaris

DORRANCE
PUBLISHING CO
EST. 1920
PITTSBURGH, PENNSYLVANIA 15238

Dorrance Publishing Co
585 Alpha Drive
Pittsburgh, PA 15238
Visit our website at *www.dorrancebookstore.com*

ISBN: 978-1-6366-1239-3
eISBN: 978-1-6366-1826-5

Foreshadowing

The young Egyptian man stood in the brisk morning air with his eyes closed, allowing the breeze to play against his face and his perceptions to only absorb the peaceful sounds of an awakening world. While he was in this meditative state was the only time in which he felt any release from the constantly thrumming and vibrating that was a constant potion of his life; this incessant throbbing, which also felt and sounded quite like the rushing of a turbulent river as far as his understanding went, the Elders had told him was simply part of his particular gift as an Oracle, and wouldn't they be so very happy to help him learn how to control this unwanted and irritating gift? Neither did he really believe in the existence of what the Elders called the *Oracles*, nor did he very much want to stay with them in Europe. He had merely accompanied them, after all, from his home across the globe because his exhaustingly exuberant father and brother had been so thrilled that there might be, finally, an explanation for his oddities. And they had urged him to accompany these people in order to *discover* his true nature, whatever that meant. That didn't sound sketchy or dangerous at all! He was fairly certain that they were eagerly seeking a way to unburden themselves of him. But his progress being with the Elders he felt was unsatisfying, for him and them. The Elders were displeased, he felt, at his adaptability to be taught, and that he often retreated outside, away from their constantly disapproving stares. *Well*, he thought, *so be it. I'll be returning home soon anyway.* This comforting thought bolstered his mind as he heard approaching footsteps, and a sarcastic sounding voice behind him saying, "There you are. It is so so *wonderful*, how you run from us and force us to waste time searching for you. If you'll come with me, we the Elders think that we've found a way to convince you to continue here with us. Do not worry, it is simply pertaining to the specification of what you said that it would take for you to be convinced that we are not lying to you for our own benefit." Wearing a determined and perturbed expression, Omage turned and strode back into the dwelling place, quickly, as if quite expecting, no *requiring*, the young man to follow him. A frustrated exhalation escaped from the younger person, but he supposed that he would have to let the Elders know sooner or later that he in no way meant to stay in their care (care? really?), so he turned and accompanied Omage inside.

The scene that he walked into in the main conference room, however, drew him up short. Pictures of four other people, of different races and ethnicities, were blown up and posted around the room, and was he seeing what was happening correctly? The Elders were hunched around these pictures wringing their hands and malevolently smiling while they whispered suspiciously to themselves. Omage turned around within the room and stated with frustration, "So. These are the other Oracles. Does this prove to you that we are not inventing this? Plans are in motion to bring these other four from around the world back here, so that we may train *all of you*, and control, no I'm sorry," Omage smiled bashfully at this, " help *you* to control your powers." The younger person recoiled from this statement. His mind reeled first with his surprise that the Elders were answering one of his questions regarding the Oracles, and if they were, what were the Elders planning to do with this!? With his heart beating increasingly rapidly, he backed towards the door. He did not very much like the thought of being used as another person's tool in their game, and warning alarms in his ears were deafening the constant buzzing that he usually heard. He wished a had some sort of weapon, a dagger even, but he was completely without anything that might be used for self-defense. The Elders seemed to read in his expression and his movement that he planned to run, and all of their focus suddenly left the pictures and turned to him. They started approaching him much like a lion might stalk its prey, but as they drew closer something extraordinary happened.

The hunted individual, as he found himself thinking of himself now, automatically feeling his mind flip back to the analytical way that he approached a hunt, much like it always did when he had been forced to go hunting gazelle and antelope with his brother. He started rapidly analyzing the room, his mind quickly running through the possible escape scenarios, since he was quite obviously the gazelle in this scenario. His mind zeroed in on the number of assailants in the room, the speed at which they were approaching him, and different ways that he thought they might attempt to subdue him. He feinted right, away from the door, and their momentary surprise at his move was all that he needed; he felt all of his awareness drive him to look at the objects which were surrounding them in the room, and while he did not actually move them, by looking at the Elders he automatically began shifting their perception of these objects. The room started warping in their minds, and they felt the very foundation of their reality suddenly not only shifting, but something like a shortage or explosion made it seem to break into glass around them. While he panted from all fours on the ground, Omage thought to himself that this was the first real manifestation of Oracle of Ether's powers, and that it was so disorganized and spotty because of inexperience. Not only should it have lasted longer, but it should not have shorted out at all. But in the split second that it took Omage to think this, the Oracle of Ether took advantage of the discombobulation of the people in the room and dashed out, running and not very much caring that he had no idea where any mode of transportation or even what sort of escape there was that he could use.

Chapter 1

Earth and Air

The sun shone down on a beautiful spring morning, complete with songbirds twittering and deer skipping through the fields of northwest Colorado; at least, that's what Hallmark would've said. Mignonne Johanson, however, paid attention to none of this. Her disgruntlement and irritation eclipsed every supposedly good facet of the morning as she attempted to work her straightening iron through her naturally curly dark brown hair without success. "Screw it," she finally breathed out, throwing the reprehensible straightening iron down on her bathroom counter. At that moment she heard, "Mignonne! Caleb! Sasha!" the voice of her overly cheery in the morning mother calling from the living room, "Better come down now, Kitty will be here any minute!" Breathe in, breathe out, be calm, Mignonne tried to repeat to herself, but her normal mantra for regaining control of herself was only partially effective this morning; she managed to grab her bookbag and march downstairs without screaming, but she still muttered and grumbled rather excessively as she worked her way down the stairs, having to use all of her focus now with avoiding being run over by her younger twin siblings as they raced downstairs, shrieking with arms and legs flying everywhere.

After Mignonne was downstairs and had grabbed an apple, she hurried out the door to wait for Kitty on the porch rather than risk being in the kitchen with the risk of the flying debris that was generated by the twins in their hunt for breakfast food. *I don't understand why they don't grow up; it's not like they're toddlers or anything*, was Mignonne's petulant thought; after all, the twins were all of nine. Closely following this thought was big sister remorse for thinking it and relief when Mignonne spotted her best friend coming up the walkway with light, dancer's motions; "Kitty! We have to get out of here quickly, before Mayhem and Disaster spot you!" Racing down the steps, Mignonne grabbed her friend's backpack and hurriedly pulled her out of the yard. "Hey, hey, slow down! Where's the flood, mi amigo?" was Kitty's only response, but she fell in step with Mignonne quickly, being used to dealing with Mignonne's drama queen mentalities. Kitty seemed to exist in a state of what could be described as perpetual chillness, being unruffled by everyday life and only exhibiting distress when things like natural disasters or weather unrest stirred her mind up to the point of extreme agitation, maybe even trauma. Fortunately, these moments were few and far between, with Mignonne being so well adjusted to Kitty's ways that she was able to see any oncoming storms in her friend and divert her away from whatever was causing the problem (sometimes this was a news reel, sometimes a severe weather forecast). Kitty lived alone with her adoptive mom, so most adults attributed Kitty's distress at these times as simple responses to the coupled trauma of being separated from her birth parents when she was barely six months old to the simple fact that her mom, Joanna Stone, while being loving and accepting of Kitty's weirdness to the extreme, existed also in a near constant state of distraction. This worked for her since she was a skilled painter and sculptor, but it maybe left something to be desired when it came to being an entirely responsive mother.

Mignonne often envied Kitty's freedom that she had at home, with no diabolical siblings or overbearing parents to deal with (especially when trying to complete such tasks as homework amidst what seemed to be a seething cauldron of turmoil). Kitty often envied Mignonne the fullness of her house, and the fact that she was very rarely alone, always having somebody to talk to when life got weird. Kitty's one relief from her near constant state of loneliness that she existed with while she was at home was her garden, which complete with succulent vegetables along with warm, colorful flowers seemed to grow under her hands without restraint. If a certain year had a drought and neighboring farmers despaired over the state of their crops, Kitty's garden stayed lush and vibrant; neighbors would ask her only partially sarcastically how much her mom was paying for the water bill, since she obviously was watering her plants under the cover of darkness away from prying eyes. Kitty would nervously giggle and blush, stammering her denial out along with a muttered string of words denying this fact and mumbling sundry other excuses for the vibrancy of her plants. Kitty found peace in her garden, away from people with their judgmental glances and snide comments; it mattered very little if these looks and observations were directed at her or not, simply being around any type of negative atmosphere was enough to drive Kitty up the wall with the inability to cope. Indeed, many people clearly remembered that when she was in her garden was the only time when Kitty wasn't about to lose it over something or another.

By the time the girls managed to successfully escape Mignonne's yard and evade her ever needy brother and sister, the talk had naturally turned the various assignments that they had in common at school; this wasn't many, since the girls had so few similar classes, being so different in their likes and abilities. For instance, Mignonne babbled on about the research paper that she was writing for her class on medieval literature (whether or not disease, such as the black plague, or rampant illiteracy contributed the most to the themes of the writing of the time period of the reign of Henry VIII; or if it was simply written in response to Henry's rampant overbearing sexual tendencies), while Kitty dreamily talked of the project that she was doing for her environmental sciences class, involving observations on what types of a particular flower would grow the best in this climate (Would the martagon lilies or the trumpet lilies grow best in this part of the world? Or maybe neither, maybe the Asiatic lilies would thrive the most in this tends-to-be-cool-and-wet environment?) Kitty's endless fascination with questions such as these caused her mom, Joanna, to shake her head and laugh, telling Mignonne that Kitty was quite obviously destined to a career in either botany or climatology. The girls might not share each other's interests, but they loved each other enough to at least attempt to ask one or two probing questions of the other person.

When the two girls walked up to the high school, for the first day of their last week there, they were assailed with chaotic emotions, ranging from relief on the part of Mignonne (sayonara, suckers!), to excitement coupled with nerves in the mind of Kitty. Mignonne seemed to take every new change in life with the ease of someone gliding along a sometimes turbulent jet stream, not being bothered by the whistling wind, but Kitty valued stability and unchanging parts of her life; perhaps this is one of the reasons why she took such comfort in her garden (it changed, certainly, but thankfully in a slow and predictable manner). Of the two girls if one of them loved change and the other sameness, they were alike in their love of other parts of life, like faithfulness in friendship, family, and most other relationships that life presented; the similarities went unnoticed by others quite often, and people would often remark in astonishment at the girls' friendship and devotion to that camaraderie. These remarks often came dripping with sarcasm and audacity, but perhaps these remarks were more of an implication of the other person's envy and longing for any relationship which had that type of continuity and trueness. But whatever the reasons for their reactions, the two trudged doggedly into the building, just in time for the first bell.

Hurrying on her way to her first class, Mignonne was accosted by a much less welcome visitor, Martin, the captain of the basketball team. "Heyyy, Nonnie!" Martin drawled out slowly, trying to keep his voice alluring and exuding a confidence that was not real; in response to his greeting Mignonne sighed and looked away, not forgetting certain activities which had occurred at a party a week ago, but not wanting to dwell on these or give Martin the wrong idea. She also slightly resented his use of the nickname that her younger siblings had come up with for her years ago, not truly disliking him as a person, but not really liking him either. Closing her eyes outside the classroom, Mignonne murmured a hurried and rather sarcastic "Hi Marty!" knowing that he detested this usage of his name. Thrown off balance a little, but with an ease that promised a good business rapport later in life, Martin recovered and leaned against the door, again trying to swagger into position. "So, we're both going away to other sides of the country soon, this is our last summer to live it up!" Martin high fived his buddy Kent who had just appeared and was trundling into the classroom. Praying for the right words so as not to give him a wrong idea of her intentions with regard to him, Mignonne forced herself to meet his gaze, which was pouring over her with an audacity only common to the high school male, "Yeah, but your summer is longer than mine; 'member I'm going to Europe for that summer work study next week?" "Oh yeah," Martin tried to hide his disappointment. "You and that freak show Kitty are both going, right?" Suddenly seething at the comment geared towards her friend, Mignonne didn't even deign to reply, but met his eyes with her own burning ones once more and then turned and marched to her desk. It was impossible to pay any attention to her math teacher because she was so worked up by Martin; besides, she was graduating in a week, what could one class period really do? But she did try to pull it together a little before the end of class, trading her anger at Martin for excitement over what she saw as her and Kitty's coming big adventure!

Meanwhile, Kitty was not faring a lot better, though her first class was probably her favorite; pottery: use the skills of the kiln to make ceramic pots and cute stone house cats! Pottery was not her favorite branch in the world of art, but she did enjoy sculpting one thing into something completely different; she found fascination in the fact that flames could be used to melt one thing and allowed for a new molding of it into something else. She was speculating on this transformation when one of her fellow art class nerds, Jamie, saw her distraction and decided to use this an opportunity to enlist Kitty's help with her coming summer project: Form a club and go after the senator through the medium of letters petitioning him to give money and manpower to the cleaning up of a local branch of river! Jamie didn't know for sure where this little riverlet came from, or whether it joined a bigger river eventually or just petered out, but she was afire with enthusiasm to get the surrounding brush cleared from around it and to get it opened up in all its miniscule glory! Jamie gushed, "Didn't Kitty, a known nature lover and conservationist, want to get it on this act, which promised to be far reaching and possibly changing to mindset of the country in regards to forestry?!" Kitty saw the real enthusiasm that Jamie spoke with, almost panting with her excitement over this project, and she was about to volunteer to help when she remembered she and Mignonne's summer trip that was coming up. "Gosh, Jamie," Kitty began a little tremulously, "I wish I could help, but you know that I'm leaving on my trip in a week. I won't be here to help most of the summer." While Kitty congratulated herself mentally for her staunch refusal (she was really trying to get better at those!), she tried not to look at Jamie's disappointed and surprised face before she slunk away to the other side of the art room. In order to keep herself from feeling guilty, Kitty ran her mind over how this miraculous trip was able to come to pass. Apparently, Kitty had a long-lost uncle who lived in Scotland and really wanted to get to know his niece and have her take part in his work for a company called Bremming & Cups, which manufactured and distributed earth friendly manufacturing equipment. While this was not really something that Kitty thought she would be really interested in, she wasn't going to pass on the opportunity to go to Europe this summer for free! Uncle Clifton insisted that she bring her friend along for the prearranged work study, so that both their mothers would feel better about the trip (even though Emma Johansen and Joanna Stone had both thoroughly checked and rechecked both the legitimacy of this company and the authenticity of this man as an actual biological relative of Kitty's; DNA records, the adoption process, and business existence and history were all thoroughly vetted by the mothers). It was with an excitement which threatened to overflow that the girls buckled into their last week at Curbman High School, trying not to let their excitement and enthusiasm completely overflow and block them from paying *a little* attention to their last week of school.

Chapter 2

Fear and Trembling

Graduation day dawned clear and stifling hot, with Mignonne kind of resenting the fact that graduation was going to be outside on the lawn and not in the air conditioned auditorium. Still, it could have been worse; like always, Kitty and Mignonne stuck together before they were forced to separate in the graduation line, and Mignonne had always seemed to have the gift of having a cool breeze generate when she needed it; she was using this strange skill, discovered by her when she was small, to keep herself and Kitty cool for as long as she could. In any event the school grounds were also nice, freshly manicured and mowed for the occasion, but Kitty couldn't help being of the opinion that it would look nicer if it was a little more wild; it seemed to chafe in its clipped and mown state, longing secretly to return to its natural state of disorder. The graduation was so long winded and mundane that Mignonne found herself longing for the end and the beginnings of post-graduation celebrations (sure to include a night which allowed her to forget the future, at least for the length of one party). Kitty and Mignonne tried to graciously accept gifts from Clark Johansen afterwards, who had tried to buy the girls graduation presents suited to their personalities; Kitty received a clay pot containing a waning hibiscus that she could return to its plant-y glory and Mignonne a signed book on wind surfing by one of the leading athletes in that field (windsurfing was something she had long been interested in, and secretly was dying to try, should she screw up her courage).

When the girls arrived back in their neighborhood, Mignonne and Kitty both saw strange shaped packages at their doors. Since they were addressed to them from Bremming & Cups Company. Mignonne assumed that they contained congratulations cards about their graduation and possibly the long-awaited plane tickets to Scotland! She was partially correct, they did contain plane tickets, but for a departure that was scheduled much sooner than anticipated, along with a telegraph in Kitty's parcel.

The telegraph read:

> *Kitty and Mignonne. Stop. There has been an emergency in the company. Stop. Chaos in everything. Stop. Need interns now, if coming at all. Stop. No time to explain further. Stop. Please see details on plane ticket. Stop. Looking forward to seeing you both. Stop.*

The tickets were for the next day, not the next week! "Well," tutted Emma Johansen, "that's a fine kettle of fish. Nobody pack anything until I check and make sure this supposed 'company crisis' is a real thing." While she investigated on the computer, Kitty and Mignonne were left in a tizzy of excitement. "Do you think this is for real," gasped Mignonne, "If it is, I so need to pack!" Kitty did not share her friend's unparalleled excitement, but instead had a nervous, almost queasy feeling in her stomach; not only would she not get a full week to adjust to the idea of going, but she wouldn't have time to prepare her garden for her long absence! Emma and Joanna came out of the house, looking resigned and crestfallen: "Okay, girls. Turns out Bremming & Cups is dealing with massive orders in their renewable eco-friendly hardware to be sent out to the aid the earthquake survivors in the Middle East; apparently, if the business doesn't start developing new ways to organize production and shipment, they might drown," was Emma Johansen slightly crestfallen response, and this was accompanied by Ms. Stone's nods and resigned smiles.

Thank goodness we made sure our passports were up to date last month, thought Mignonne, always of a more practical nature than her "eyes on the heavens" friend; Kitty simply tittered and started bouncing up and down with nerves, excusing herself to go back to the miniscule cottage that she lived in with Joanna, using finishing her packing as a pretty reliable excuse to escape questions and comments from the peanut gallery of her mom and Mrs. Johansen. Since her parents kindly kept the twins out of her room while she worked, Mignonne finished putting the last of her two suitcases together and sat down on the edge of the same bed that she'd occupied since she outgrew her crib, albeit with a new mattress; surprisingly, she felt herself tearing up when she stopped and faced the reality of leaving everything she was familiar with, including the safety ballast of her parents and the oddly comforting, sometimes (if not experiencing some sort of fiasco), twins. The thought of leaving home and going somewhere where she wouldn't have to watch her step at home as if she was on a game safari and was evading curious beasts was truthfully quite frightening when she really stopped and thought about it. Yes, Mignonne loved change and new horizons, but this was really going to be a big new horizon! *Pull it together,* Mignonne thought to herself, and forced her mind to think only about the super coolness of this trip and nothing else; amidst this reverie Mignonne spared a thought wondering how Kitty was processing this new information that had so unexpectedly come to light.

Kitty herself was trying to figure out how she was dealing with this new development along the path of her life; true, getting to go one week earlier on her trip wasn't exactly mind blowing, but Kitty found that being able to take things slowly and steadily helped her to wrap her mind more easily around occurrences. Pondering this while attempting to pull a brush through her wavy, almost honey colored hair, it occurred to her that the place where she did her best thinking was very accessible. Going to her garden was the place that allowed to clear her mind of endless possibilities, of jumbled and conflicting ideas and thoughts, to really feel free and unrestrained. *Yes, I will head outside, sit on my bench, and try and chill;* with this thought Kitty marched into her tiny kitchen, made herself a cup of tea, and took it out to one of her favorite spots, a wrought iron bench located so conveniently in her garden, under the spreading branches of a willow that lived in the corner, tucked away next to her neighbors' surrounding stone fence. While she was sitting on her bench with her tea, Kitty tried to work out if she could handle this sudden development; before she could panic outright, thankfully Joanna Stone was using her radar sense for crisis in her child, finely honed throughout the years of dealing with Kitty. And she quietly made her way outside, sitting beside Kitty on the bench, not saying anything immediately but just letting the conversation arise naturally. Unable to hold her emotions in anymore, Kitty looked at Joanna with pleading eyes, scarcely able to keep the waterworks from overflowing onto her cheeks since she was so overwhelmed with these new emotions. "Mom?" Kitty began tentatively, unsure of what to say next; she met Joanna's nonjudgmental, gentle eyes and gathered a little courage from them. "Do you think this is a good idea? I mean, going across the world into who knows what?" If Kitty was secretly hoping that Joanna would say, 'You're right Kitty; this is a bad idea, I don't think you or Mignonne should go,' she was to be disappointed. Joanna Stone met her gaze and spoke her words with confidence: "I think that this is a very good idea, Kitty. At what other part of your life, like when you're tied down with either work or a family of your own will you be able to go off and do something like this? Emma Johansen and I have checked and rechecked the legitimacy of this whole thing, and if someone from your biological family wants to get to know you, I can't begrudge them that opportunity. Yes, I'll miss you dearly, a lot like Mignonne's family will miss her, but God brought you into my life from around the world when you were a baby, and I have no doubt that God will bring you safely back to me after your wild ride." Her mother's sincerity and peace breathed out with every word, and Kitty felt a new courage blossoming inside her chest. Kitty breathed out with relief, closed her eyes, and said with new confidence, "If that's the case, Mom, then don't you think that we could use a little more tea while we watch our favorite meaningless sitcom together for the last time for a little while?" Kitty tried to speak like she had confidence, to convince her mom with but more importantly, to convince herself with. Kitty and Joanna ambled slowly back into the kitchen, putting more tea water on to boil, and trying to find the comfiest positioning on the couch with which to enjoy one of their mutual senseless pleasures on TV.

The next day dawned a little cloudy and humid, appearing kind of sad to see Kitty and Mignonne go, and so being petulant and not sharing any good weather with sunshine and breezes. This actually did make it a little easier to go through with the process though, for all involved, and it was with determination that the girls hugged Mr. Johansen, who had kindly given them a ride to the airport on his way to work. They checked their parcels in and got in line preparing to show their boarding passes. Eyeing the two girls when their turn came up in line, the attendant checked their tickets with their driver's licenses; apparently deciding that Kitty was the less (marginally) intimidating of the two, he cut her a smile, one that was intended to through the medium of a smirk, tell Kitty of his availability and his interest in getting to know her better. Ignoring the increasingly disgruntled line behind Mignonne and Kitty, the young man cut his eyes in Kitty's direction, complimenting his smirk with vocal attempts at being enticing; "Sooo, Miss Kitty, I don't see kind of interesting last names like yours often…" "What, you don't see the name Stone often?" Mignonne cut in, impatient to be on the plane and away from the growing mutinous looks that were coming from the line behind them. The dude angrily cut his eyes in Mignonne's direction, wanting to regain his control of the situation and put Mignonne in her place: "No, *ma'am*, I wasn't just talking about 'Stone.'" Turning his gaze back to less hostile place of Kitty's face, in an attempt to really be a smooth talker, he entirely altered his tone and said, " On your license it says 'Mun-Stone' that's kind of cool; hyphenated names aren't as common for girls your age... So, is there a story attached to that?" The attendant was devoutly hoping that wasn't her maiden name hyphenated with her married name... She didn't look old enough to be married but with the weird people that he saw on a daily basis, you couldn't be sure. Before Kitty could respond, a portly man brandishing a clipboard yelled, "Steven! What's the hold up? We have a line forming, bud!" before he left amid the scattered thanksgiving of the crowd. Smiling sadly Steven looked once more at Kitty and said while trying again to speak seductively, "I hope to see you when you come back, beautiful," and motioning them onboard the plane. Mignonne and Kitty had little trouble finding their seats, in spite of rampant fits of giggling and Kitty's shy blushing. Actually, really thankful for this distraction from her nerves, Kitty settled back into her seat and pondered once more the oddity of her name. "Stone" of course came from her adoptive mom, but since Joanna did not want to entirely cut Kitty's past family out of her life, she decided long ago to include Kitty's given name, "Mun," odd-weird as it was. She didn't think the six month old little girl would ever care either way, but it was safer to cover her bases in case a teenage Kitty pulled away from her and used the separation of her current life with her life history as an excuse to leave home and end her relationships with her adoptive mother.

Not suffering from profound questions involving hyphens, names, or family history, Mignonne contentedly put in the complimentary plane ear buds and settled down to watch a movie on the little screen in front of her seat. The differences between domestic flights and international flights were profound, she reflected, as she opened and enjoyed her complimentary fruit cup. She wasn't in any high class seat, simple business class, but if she didn't know any better she would think she'd been upgraded to poshy poshy first class. Spending a great deal of time thinking about the socio-economic framework of the body of the plane allowed her time not to think about what would happen when they arrived in Scotland. She assumed that Uncle Mephistopheles, her nickname for their benefactor Kitty's uncle, would either meet them himself, or (scarier), would send a company car and driver. How would they know they were getting in the right car, if this was the case?! What if a random abductor appeared and used his finely honed skills as a smooth talker to get them in the car? Or, thinking about it, she had no idea what Uncle Mephistopheles looked like. The picture of him on the company website was miniscule and little blurry, and until this very moment this hadn't bothered her. Why hadn't she and Kitty insisted on receiving a full size family portrait of this man, for crying out loud?! Fighting encroaching spurts of hyperventilation, she shot Kitty a look; *look at Kitty*, she thought, *so serene and unencumbered by these obviously problematic musings, smiling faintly while she gazed out the window at the clouds*. "Kitty!" Mignonne tried to shriek but only succeeded in squeaking, "I just thought of some absolutely essential questions that I have to ask you!!!" The girls got down to analyzing each request, ranging as far as wondering if the uncle was a world famous movie star who would meet them in his stretch limousine (did Scotland have stretch limos?) to wondering if this "company" was really a front for the international sex trade, and the uncle had spent a great deal of money on really nice plane tickets to bring his prey into his own hands. If Mrs. Johansen hadn't so thoroughly vetted him, Mignonne might seriously think so. After reminding herself of this, Mignonne tried to focus on her first order of business prior to arriving in Scotland: remember that Uncle Mephistopheles' name was really Uncle Clifton Mayor; in her opinion that was just as weird, but what are you gonna do? *C'est la vie*.

Chapter 3

Upgraded Fear and Trembling

If Kitty had thought she was nervous before they left, and even more nervous on the plane, when someone with a Scottish accent announced over the intercom that, *"Aire luchd-siubhail! Welcome passengers! We are about to enter Glasgow Airport and land in the terminal there! As the plane descends, please remain seated and buckled in! Once the plane comes to a stop, please grab any and all of your possessions and prepare to get in line and disembark the aircraft! Thank you for flying Air Scotland!"* Mignonne also was trying really hard not to engage in Lamaze breathing, reminding herself over and over again how excited she supposedly was; *remember how great you felt last week at home thinking about this trip?! Remember, bitch!* The girls finally managed to depart from the plane with these thoughts, and with less turmoil than one might expect given the circumstances. The first order of business was to hope and pray that their baggage would be on the revolving carousel and not left stranded in the airport back home. After showing the attendant (Scottish this time!) their passports and IDs once again upon landing upon ye olde sod (Mignonne had tried on the flight to memorize a booklet that was supposedly full of fun Scottish phrases), Kitty and Mignonne found their bags and then made their way to the front entrance of the terminal, trying to disguise their fear at being in a strange country with no known help coming as the blasé attitude that would be typical for young globetrotting hotties (they guessed). Thankfully, a gentleman who looked alarmingly like the fuzzy shot online that they'd seen approached them not to long after.

"You must be Kitty!" the man exclaimed awkwardly, not entirely concealing his discomfort in being in such a place which was crawling with huge amounts of people from every spot on the globe. Kitty's brain raced as she tried to decide whether to greet her long lost uncle with a hug or a typical nervous American wave; she had almost decided on the hug when she was saved as Uncle Clifton turned to Mignonne; "You most decidedly are Mignonne! I'd know you anywhere!" Immediately filing away in her brain how strange it was that Uncle Clifton didn't seem to speak with a Scottish accent, but rather one that made her remember movies that she'd seen on TV about the Arabian life that featured characters speaking with Egyptian *Masry*, Mignonne automatically extended her hand, thanking years of parental training on "how you greet older strangers" for this impulse. Still, Uncle Clifton rather awkwardly attempted to shake her hand, not seeming used to this action, and then using an unknown language directed the men who were accompanying him to get Mignonne's and Kitty's bags, ushering the girls out of the airport and into a waiting car. Not a limousine, but still a nice car. Once Uncle Clifton was seated up front with the driver while Kitty and Mignonne occupied the backseat, he turned to them and let out a breath which could have been a sigh of relief before he started speaking.

"So, ladies," he began, trying to punctuate his words with his "I'm awkward around people" smile, "I cannot tell you the consuming joy that I feel in having you two here with me. Perhaps you ladies would care for a beverage? Ginger ale or sparkling water, pray tell?" Uncle Clifton was such an odd mix of out-of-place coupled with a face that

Mignonne could not convince herself was only forty-five (as his website claimed), that Mignonne was momentarily speechless, only able to nod and accept a glass of Perrier. Apparently cat also had Kitty's tongue after this question was asked, with her mind racing amidst her observations that this gentleman first of all did not sound Scottish (as he claimed to be), and secondly that his discomfort even being here in the car *could* be attributed to the strangeness of meeting his long separated niece and her friend, but somehow Kitty didn't think that this was it. There appeared to be worlds of thoughts swirling around his head, behind his dark brown eyes, and Kitty couldn't help but think that he had a great deal to share with them should he choose to trust them. Maybe this kind of wariness came from running an international environmentally geared shipping company, and all the bizarreness that had to bring, but Kitty just wasn't sure. Bells were going off in her head; fortunately not the *You're in imminent danger* bells, but bells nonetheless. The late afternoon sunlight was growing soft as the car pulled into the long, curved driveway of a regal late century castle that had obviously been refurbished into a few hotel suites, for the few more posh visitors that this region of Scotland entertained annually.

Mignonne felt her heart rate accelerate as the car came to a stop in front of the old-school castle, anxiety beginning to truly confront her mind, since she hadn't really been expecting to be taken to a hotel. She wasn't sure exactly what she had been expecting, but this bothered her. As her heartbeat went like a trip, she caught Kitty's eyes, hoping that her nervousness, which was quickly accelerating into a fever pitch, wasn't visible to their driver or their host. Unfortunately, this did little to calm her nerves, as Kitty's gaze was just as full of fear as she was sure her own was. The driver opened the doors of the backseat, but Kitty and Mignonne were still too paralyzed to step out of the car. Seeming to sense their nerves, Uncle Clifton smiled awkwardly and motioned them forward, his voice trying to remain calm as he said, "The lobby of this establishment will serve for our purposes of communication; please come in with me." Figuring that at least this was a public place bound to have other members of civilian life, Mignonne got out of the car, holding onto the car roof to keep her knees from buckling. Once Kitty had taken courage from Mignonne's movement and departed from her own seat, Uncle Clifton motioned for the driver to take the car away and led the girls across the gravel pathway leading up to the front doors. Seeming a little confused by the revolving door at the entrance, Uncle Clifton finally leapt forward in the carousel of glass hatches, apparently knowing a little of the lay-out of the hotel, because he glanced at the person working the front desk. The person leapt into motion, wringing his hands and simpering as he motioned the party of three into an elegant, but drafty, side room with a broad table that was quite obviously reserved for business meetings or high paying liaisons. The room seemed to exude a not muted form of sophistication, from the damask and velvet chairs to the rich carpets that were laid over the stone floor. The hotel attendant rushed around turning a few desk lamps on, then ran out promising to return with tea. A fire was crackling in one of the far corners, adding a little warmth to the almost cold room, and Uncle Clifton motioned the girls to be seated around a small table right in front of it. Sitting in a close by antique wing chair, Uncle Clifton breathed in and met the frantic eyes of the girls, smiling a little and speaking slowly, choosing his words with care.

"Well ladies, the three of us have much to discuss; I made the reservations at this location so that we might be able to speak without being disturbed, hopefully in a setting that is less frightening than others, as our words are going to naturally contain some iotas of fear, especially with regard to you two personally". *What the hell*, Mignonne thought frantically, but before she could muster any words the attendant returned, bearing in shaking hands a tray containing a pot of tea and several small pastries, thankfully being able to keep it steady enough to successfully lower the tray onto the table. Uncle Clifton then indicated by a brisk motion of his hand that the server should leave, which the man did with no hesitation, bowing hastily and almost skipping out of the room. Not even trying any longer to keep up his friendly ruse, Uncle Clifton, who was quite obviously used to commanding and ordering people, motioned to the plate, sighed, and stated, "Please eat, girls, and we will begin." Mignonne sensed a strange reluctance to talk about whatever was coming and also a driving necessity to get the words out in Uncle Clifton's manner, but at this point her head was ringing with nerves and it was with difficulty that she didn't run from the room. Kitty, on the other hand, appeared to have decided to practice some form of zen meditation, and unlike Mignonne was able to look without fear directly into Uncle Clifton's eyes, seeming to almost challenge him with her own eyes into speaking.

Chapter 4

Say What?

Clearly surprised by Kitty's thinly veiled hostility, Uncle Clifton shifted a little in his seat and tried to keep his voice calm as he began. "I'm supposing, probably correctly, that they two of you know little or nothing about ancient lore in general?" Kitty and Mignonne didn't know what to say; obviously they had studied some Native American legends in school but that was about it in regards to anything, and they didn't understand what this question could have to do with anything that was currently happening. Not seeming to be expecting a response, Uncle Clifton continued on doggedly. "I'm quite sure that the two of you have ascertained that while I do have much to tell you, I do not in fact own any shipping/printing company and I am not in least bit concerned about said company's impact on the environment," Uncle Clifton said, a tiny bit more naturally, smiling a little as he did so. "You two are in fact not here in order to take part in this alleged company's foray into the global initiative. But I did bring you two her for an important reason." *What the crap is he talking about?* thought Mignonne, as her mind was quickly making a turn into fight-or-flight mode as she frantically half-stood and tried to determine where the exit was. Kitty also couldn't even imagine what Uncle Clifton had in mind if it was different from what he wrote to them in his letters, but she had seen enough *Dateline* to know that it was a girl's worst nightmare to have gone across the world from home to meet a basically complete stranger and to have no viable form of communication to the outside world (At this castle outpost on the other side of the planet her cell phone had no bars; she wasn't sure if Mignonne's did. And Kitty desperately tried to come up with a way to get Mignonne alone.). Mignonne was suddenly desperately thirsty but too afraid to drink from the inviting tea on the tray; what if the waiter-dude was in on this whole conspiracy? What if he, in actuality, was the head of this operation? In a small portion of her brain Mignonne knew that these were wild thoughts and that the attendant probably wasn't, in fact, in on anything, but in the dominant part of her mind she was desperately grasping at any conclusion to give meaning to this situation. Seeing Mignonne's panic, Kitty put on a tone of false bravado and chirped in Uncle Clifton's general direction, "Then you'd better start telling us something that makes some kind of sense or we're out." She wasn't absolutely sure where they could go or if she and Mignonne could escape and try to somehow return home, but she was willing to go off the possibility of being able to do so. After all, they had American passports, cell phones, and credit cards at their disposal. Kitty tried to tell herself that many people had done more with less. Kitty was trying to fool herself into thinking with calmness about what was developing into true panic, but her false sense of security was fading fast.

All of the many years of their friendship Kitty and Mignonne naturally learned to balance each other out and to know intuitively when the other person was approaching a mental meltdown. Gaining confidence listening to Kitty's strong words, but knowing how empty they probably were, Mignonne stood up all the way. Uncle Clifton also stood, putting his hands palms open in front of him. Breathing quickly he started out with, "Girls, girls, I promise that I have no negative intentions or plans for the two of you in mind. I simply want to explain to you something that I believe will be of interest to you. If it is not then I will have you two driven back to airport myself," he began by talking pretty quickly but by the end of his statement had returned to his signature slow and meticulous brand of talking. Not knowing what else to do, and being so totally out of her element, Mignonne sat down quickly and stared at Uncle Clifton, swearing to herself that if he didn't start making sense soon, they were outta there. Lowering his hands and slowly returning to his seat, Uncle Clifton began once more, trying to speak calmly but with definite growing irritation at all that had happened up to this point. "Alright then, if we can maintain some order of calm for the rest of this talk that would be splendid, as I have little intention of remaining here in this drafty castle all night. I'm going to assume that you two know nothing, and so I will start at the beginning of a story that is almost as old as creation". He paused then, steepling his fingers in front of his face before he began again. "I assume once again that the two of you are familiar at least in general with the story that is contained in Genesis, in the Hebrew Torah; this account begins with the words, 'In the beginning God created the Heavens and the Earth' and so forth and so on, but the gospel writer John actually comes a little closer to what was meant by this, that God created a new way and realm of being out of the infinity of His own being. John says that in the beginning was the Word, which is a multifaceted prism of consciousness and awareness that God is, through this plethora of facets, like the surface of a diamond, God breathed creation into being, giving to it an endless amount of areas that the Light can shine off of and produce different colors and effects. This new world that was created began to split and slide apart on its own, and so God gave to it dimensions and regulatory devices with which to order itself and not to fly apart at the smallest injunction. These, so to speak, regulatory tools and devices are what I have gathered the two of you here today to discuss.

Looking across the bridge of his nose, Uncle Clifton slowed down and spoke as if talking to a foreigner who you were not certain spoke the same language: "You two know what the elements are, I am presuming?" Feeling disgruntled but still a little intrigued, Mignonne stated without pausing "Well yeah… they're the parts of the world that 'cannot be reduced to any portion smaller than itself' and some such. They are the most foundational parts of existence. There's a lot of them," she said, pausing at this point and telling herself that high school science was at least serving *some* purpose. "Yes, well," started Uncle Clifton with only marginally less irritation, "while that is true, I was actually talking in particular about the original elements; what humankind thought of for eons as the basic building blocks of existence: earth, fire, water, wind, and ether. The elements that form the center of human life, and so all life on all of the planet in some sense or another. Out of the chaos that came with the beginning of creation, these elements proved to be the most difficult to contain and to be absolutely essential to establishing and maintaining order. In the Elder scrolls it says that human guardians were given to each of these elements, so that regulation and established peace might be maintained. The individuals who guard and direct these elements only emerge when the world is threatening to enter into a state of chaos; sometimes one generation might have or not have what the Elder scrolls call 'oracles,' a term that has come to mean something entirely different in recent years in layman's terms, but which denotes these guardians. However, knowing well the human propensity for creating negative balance, I am not surprised that most generations of humanity do have these individuals. Humans seem to be intent on seeing how far they can push the world before it topples over, so the oracles are very often necessary to maintain balance. I am one of the Elders who watch and wait for the individuals, hoping that they will emerge, and we thought that this generation would not have the oracles until the order of the Elders came across, quite by accident, the oracle of ether. Five years ago, he was one of our initiates, and we were training him to follow in our ancient and hallowed footsteps. Of course, once we learned what he was, we had to attempt to let him know without causing undue trauma. But he departed from us, panicking after finding out who he is after years of studying the purpose and abilities of the oracles, thinking them to be a completely esoteric group, never fathoming how someone like him could be one of them.

"That is an over simplified explanation of these mind-blowing ideas; I am certain that question upon question is circulating in your minds, and my driver will be another hour getting here to whisk me away. Please, don't be afraid, but ask." These words acted as if he'd made a perfectly mundane conjecture, pretending that he had just asked them a trivial question, such as "Where do you want to go on vacation?" and not said something so out of this world with them. Neither Kitty nor Mignonne was immediately available to know what to say. Finally, her mind deciding that this was a sick joke that someone had invested a lot of time and money into, for a reason that she could not fathom, Mignonne managed to stutter out the question, "You really expect us, two girls from the States whose greatest life question has been, 'What should I have for breakfast before I go to school?' to believe that any of this is even conceivably real or has anything to do with us? Why did you pay to have us flown all of the way around the world to tell us this bogus junk? Might be interesting if we were watching a late night documentary on TV with nothing else to do, but seriously? Why lie in the letters about why we were coming to Scotland? You could have said, 'Dear Kitty and Mignonne: I want to pay to have you flown in on your last summer after high school so that I can feed the two of you a story that makes absolutely no sense and has no relevance for anything.' That would make more sense to me." Finally huffing back in her seat, Mignonne refused to continue to be a part of this discussion. "Mignonne," Uncle Clifton started to say, "I have no interest in trying to convince the two of you of anything. We can continue this discussion tomorrow after the two of you have had a good night's sleep. I have already reserved the two of you a room for the night at this establishment, and I expect that you will find this acceptable." You could say that "he said and vanished," but that would be a much more subtle version of what happened; he stood, looking highly displeased at how this whole conversation had gone, turned on his heel, and stalked out of the room, leaving Kitty and Mignonne starring after him and looking at one another in disbelief. "I really have no idea what to say," murmured Kitty through thinly veiled tears welling in her eyes. "I really thought that this was going to be a great working opportunity for the two of us; plus, I thought it might be a good way for me to connect with my birth family for the first time. I doubt that guy was even my uncle though, or that his name is 'Clifton.' This is so messed up, I'm so sorry that I dragged you into this, Miggy." At this point Kitty began quietly crying, hanging her head down, and letting her thick, auburn-honey hair hang over her face and shield her from visibility. Mignonne, for the sake of her friend, made herself regain the powers of volatilization; she turned to Kitty and sighed: "I'm not mad at you, Kitty. You couldn't have known anything would be as weird and awkward as all of this has been; personally I'm relieved that your faux-uncle hasn't made a obvious motion to sell us into sex slavery or anything, though I wouldn't put it past him to have us stay somewhere that specializes in underage promiscuity. Let's just go to our room and try to get some sleep before we make him take us back to the airport tomorrow; assuming, of course, that this place has 'rooms' with beds and hopefully hot showers." The squirrelly worker bustled back into the room, stopping short when he saw Kitty and Mignonne's distress but quickly regaining composure of himself, chalking it up to American drama. He stuttered, "Please, ladies, follow me to your room; your bags have already been brought up by staff." Shaking her head in bafflement, Mignonne stood and she and Kitty followed the attendant, not to an elevator but to a vast flight of stairs that looked to consist of some of the original woodwork of the manor house, knowing by glancing at some of the travel posters in the lobby that this was not in fact a castle but simply a lordly old estate. Thanking her mother for her insistence on extreme cardio as a workout regimen, Kitty climbed the stairs and followed the gentleman to a room located off the middle of one of the tower-looking buildings that were part of the house; little squirrelly helper man then bowed out and left the girls alone in the bedrooms with their luggage. Mignonne was immensely relieved once again to see their suitcases, taking this opportunity to put on her pajamas; she considered going to the adjoining bathroom and brushing her teeth, but frankly her mind was in too much of a tizzy to even seriously consider such a thing. Promising herself that she would brush extra hard in the morning, Mignonne climbed into one of the two elegant four poster beds in the room, making sure that she left bedroom slippers close to her bed in case she had to get up and go to the bathroom. The stone floor was desperately cold on her feet. Thankful that at least she and Kitty didn't appear to be in any eminent danger, Mignonne curled up in the bed and surrendered herself to oblivion.

Kitty had long envied Mignonne the ease with which she was able to fall asleep; hurricanes, tornadoes, close wildfires, these mean nothing with regards to how quickly Mignonne fell asleep every night. Kitty, though she changed into her pajamas and climbed into the other bed, restlessly tossed and turned on the obnoxiously nice sheets; she supposed that any resentment that she felt towards the sheets was really animosity for her 'uncle's' having tricked her and Mignonne so decidedly. In order to quiet her mind, she wondered what her mother would be doing right about now; she wasn't entirely certain about how the time change would work, but assumed that Joanna was in bed asleep, hopefully peacefully, or preparing for her lecture at the community college where she taught botany for the next day. Maybe she would be working in the garden at their house, happily remembering her students' quips or wondering what Kitty was doing on her world adventure. It didn't feel much like an adventure at this point, thought Kitty; more like thinking that you won the lottery only to find the winnings all came in Monopoly money. Disappointing, and even, dare she think it, infuriating. How dare Uncle Clifton drag them all across the ocean to feed them a ridiculous story that had no relevance to their lives!? Only, she hardly dared to consider this, what if it did have relevance? The oracle of ether (whatever the heck that was) hadn't known he was an oracle until the Elders had told him, Uncle Clifton had said; but Kitty felt sure that if she was a weird natural witch of any elements that she would know by now. Making a note to herself to look up the word 'ether' on her phone tomorrow, Kitty eventually was able to quiet her mind enough to fall into light, but fortunately dreamless, sleep.

Chapter 5

It Gets Weirder

The next morning dawned with weather that was nothing to write home about; not particularly warm but not technically cold, with a weak sun attempting to shine through onto the coarse moors. And Mignonne and Kitty were awakened by a female worker knocking on their door and announcing that she had some porridge for them for breakfast, featuring lovely roast *isag* and toast. Wishing fervently for some coffee to accompany her porridge and baked fish *(who has baked fish for breakfast?)*, Mignonne got up and let the bustling Scottish *bean-phosda* into the room, where the lady quickly sat the tray on a writing desk and quickly hurried out, muttering about lazy late sleeping American lasses. Rousing herself in response to the quite nice smells coming from the breakfast tray, Kitty shuffled over to join Mignonne in partaking of what was actually a pretty good breakfast, all things considered. The steaming pot of Gaelic coffee which came on the tray looked inviting, and Mignonne eagerly poured herself a cup, thinking that at least she would be well caffeinated for the horrors of the day. Not remembering that most Scottish/Gaelic coffee comes preflavored with alcohol, Mignonne eagerly drank her cup, only wondering afterwards what the strange taste in her mouth was. Kitty, not being a coffee lover, drank a glass of fresh milk from local Highland cattle who spent their days roaming the hills and taking selfies for Scottish websites. The girls had never had porridge technically, but found it to be quite nice and very similar to more traditional American fare such as oatmeal. Finishing her breakfast, Mignonne forced herself to ask Kitty what the plans for the day were, or if there *were* any plans. "Yes, I think so; Uncle Clifton said something about coming back today after we'd been able to sleep and process everything that he told us," Kitty mumbled, looking incredulously at Mignonne while she finished her toast. "Well, that's just great," huffed Mignonne. "But if he doesn't show up by 2 o'clock, I vote that we try to get some sort of transportation and go back to the airport. I guess a horse or something would do," Mignonne tacked on at the end, smiling bashfully at Kitty, wanting to make the events of last night into not-a-big-deal, even if she was only fooling herself. Kitty rolled her eyes as she pulled on a pair of hiking books that she had wisely brought to Scotland, not knowing what the day would bring but knowing that there are few occasions where stilettos are called for and that this most likely wasn't one of them.

Unsure of what exactly to do, Kitty and Mignonne loitered in their room for a little while, and then started thinking that perhaps Uncle Clifton would meet them downstairs. The girls embarked on the somewhat perilous journey down the ancient stone stairs into the lobby area, where not knowing what to do Kitty pulled out her sketchbook and started idly sketching birds and plants, while Mignonne sat down to read a book that was lying on the coffee table. It happened to be one that she had enjoyed growing up, entitled *Kidnapped* by Robert Louis Stevenson. Thankful to lose herself even for a brief minute in a nautical world, Mignonne dove into the book; she and Kitty were left undisturbed for a few minutes, until the person who was working the front desk, who happened to be a different person than yesterday, started up nervously and started anxiously wringing her hands while attempting to glance unnoticed at the entrance of Uncle Clifton. Passing by the attendant, Uncle Clifton moved unobtrusively into the sitting room. Mignonne and Kitty only noticed him when he sat down in a chair that was directly opposite from them and noisily cleared his throat. Fighting waves of irritation at his remembered absurdity, Mignonne closed and put down the book, and Kitty looked up from her sketchpad. "Well, ladies," flaunting his newly regained poise, Uncle Clifton deigned to say, "I trust your night was pleasant. I came back today to continue telling you my so-called 'absurd' story about the oracles and their place and purpose in this life. Mayhaps it would be best if I tell you about how the Elders, for centuries, have tracked down and brought the oracles together. But I cannot share these things at this public location. Perhaps the two of you would like to accompany me elsewhere?" Before the girls could reply, quite possibly by giving him a decided 'no,' Uncle Clifton broke back in. "I am aware that the two of you are most likely made uncomfortable in my presence, especially after the negative response that the two of you had to all that I told you last night… It is quite alright if we go together to a place that is still public, but that affords us a greater degree of solitude." Looking at each other, Mignonne and Kitty exchanged bewildered glances, but in the end curiosity about what this freak-show of a man had left to tell them won out. Kitty glanced at Mignonne, who answered the glance with a sardonic half-smile and nodded slightly. Breathing deeply, taking time to gather her words and her certainty about her answer, Kitty eventually met the eyes of her alleged uncle and also nodded slowly. "Very well," quoth Uncle Clifton, "Then let us proceed; I noticed a somewhat charming little corner park not far from this location. I feel sure that you, Kitty, at least will be more comfortable there." Without another word, Uncle Clifton turned and exited more adeptly this time through the revolving doors, being followed by the person who had driven them all last night. Mignonne considered him to be a part of Uncle Clifton's *entourage*, for lack of a better descriptive word with which to define him in her head. Kitty and Mignonne followed Uncle Clifton out the door, devoutly hoping that this supposed park was not far and was very public.

Struggling to keep up with Uncle Clifton's brisk pace, the girls were forced to follow him at a trot, with Kitty very relieved that they were not heading towards any car that was evident but were rather walking with great speed towards a place that she had not noticed the night before: a quaint little park which was bordered by lots of trees and had cute little flower beds scattered throughout that was located about a block and a half from the lodge. A little sitting area made up of a white bench and two matching chairs was located not far off the main road bordering the hotel. And it was to here that Uncle Clifton led the girls. The park was so pleasing with smells and sights of the natural world that Kitty found herself involuntarily smiling a little, noticing with pleasure that the garden wasn't really formally laid out, but that some freedom of movement had been left for the growing things which were present. Less impressed with the park overall, Mignonne walked forward huffily and claimed the little white bench as her whole seating space, with Kitty gingerly perching on one of the chairs and Uncle Clifton even more gingerly settling back into the other chair. Taking a deep breath, with closed eyes, Uncle Clifton finally looked at the girls and said, "Let us begin."

"I have a question for the two of you," Uncle Clifton started, with authority but also with what Mignonne perceived as contrived patience; "Has either one of you even given some thought into the possible veracity of what I told you two last night? Because the bizarre nature that you found in my words is about to get even stranger, and it will be helpful if the two of you have at least attempted to see some truth in what I said." Finally, totally losing patience with this man, Mignonne closed her eyes and in a slow, measured, but still deadly manner uttered the words, "Well sure, Uncle Clifton, because everything that you said last night makes perfect sense if simply, rationally considered. I mean, who could possibly invent a long and sordid story about mystical beings endowed for the protection of the earth with supernatural abilities? I mean, who wouldn't believe that?" To her surprise, Uncle Clifton actually genuinely smiled at this somewhat sarcastic statement: "Good, good. Human beings are only able to make sarcastic comments based at least a little bit on what we believe to be truth; if we do not have a perceived level of truth that we accept we are unable to form necessary sarcastic comments about said topic. And so, let us begin with the more pertinent aspects of this discussion." Settling back again into his chair, Uncle Clifton finally began.

"First of all, my formal name is not 'Uncle Clifton,' although the two of you are welcome to continue calling me this if it would make things easier for you. The order to which I belong, have belonged since before breath entered my lungs for the first time, you can recall, as I stated last night, 'the Elders.' It is our mission to seek out and work with the oracles, should they be present in any given generation, helping them to recognize and learn to effectively utilize their 'gifts.' I told you briefly about the oracle of ether that the Elders identified five years ago, but who has subsequently disappeared from our order and is currently galivanting across the far reaches of this planet." "Hold up," Mignonne broke in, "you say that you 'identified' the oracle of ether, but how in the world did you do this? I mean, problem one: finding a supposed 'oracle' *physically*; problem two: figuring out who the oracle is and then figuring out that that person is really who you're looking for? That seems to be kind of a far stretch to go on, even supposing that these people really exist." Seeming almost happy with Mignonne's level of determination with finding the truth out, but still irritated with her interruption, Uncle Clifton cleared his throat, closed his eyes, and softly prayed *Please grant me patience, oh Yahweh*, before reopening his eyes. And, with his own level of determination, forcing himself to be calm as he continued. "All of your questions, valid as they are, will be answered in the correct order of proceedings that we are taking part in here; I promise to answer all that is giving you pause, only I will do so at the right time. Since you two seem to be so determined to find out every little detail, I will tell you that in the history of the Elders many years have been spent in developing tools that will give a fairly accurate reading on the presence of an oracle using their abilities, intentionally or otherwise. It does not specifically identify a person for us, but it charts the location of the usage of power on something akin to a charting sonography. This is in several ways very similar to how the National Earthquake Information Center tracks and gives information on forthcoming earthquakes to the concerned area or region, warning them of subsequent seismic activity. Like the NEIC, our data software, for lack of a better name, is able to identify and give a fairly accurate placement of cause. This even goes so far as to give us a specific window of people who have might have caused this activity. We send out seekers towards these pictures, and once this seeker is in close location to the activity, other data will be examined in order to show us specifically who we are seeking. But to return to my first point, the name that was given to me by the Elders, and which most people know me, is Omage, and I serve the order through my services as seeker."

Head spinning wildly as she attempted to keep up with what this not right-in-the-head person who saying, Mignonne stared ahead and tried to form another question: "But, but… okay, correct me if I'm wrong, but seekers are sent out to supposedly find and so to speak 'bring into the fold' these oracles; why are you looking into us? We're not 'oracles,' or I feel sure that we would know by now. So thanks for dragging us across the world for no reason." Shaking her head in confusion, Mignonne stood up at this point, desperately trying to escape the situation because she had a feeling that this was about to get really, really weird, and her rational mind rebelled against it. Quite frankly she did not really want to hear any more.

Kitty looked at Mignonne in bewilderment, clearly wondering where she was trying to go after they had agreed between themselves to at least hear Uncle Clifton out. Grabbing Mignonne's elbow, she turned to Omage and blurted out, "She's right; why?" Her words were not as technically specific as Mignonne's maybe, but they carried the same weight of meaning, still containing the same level of insistence and necessity. Omage leaned forward in his chair, endeavoring to contain his excitement as he avowed with purposeful tone, "You are very right in asking that question, Mignonne. My order has reason to believe that one, or quite possibly, both of you are members of this highly specific class. That is why I asked that the two of you come to meet me here, in this entirely neutral zone, rather than at the home of the Elders in Africa. Unfortunately, we are forced to think about the lower level of the political climate in our seeking, and it occurred to me that two young girls were not likely to travel to Africa in meeting with or possibly working with someone who is practically a stranger." "No practically about it," mumbled Mignonne, resenting more and more the fact that this man did not seem to answer particular questions, but rather to skirt around them, only supplying answers after much deliberation. "Ah," Omage said smiling, "You must try not to be too annoyed with me, Mignonne, as I truly have only your best interests in mind. I have reason to believe that the two of you possess and have unconsciously been demonstrating the skills of the oracles without realizing this, inadvertently creating small vibrations in the balance of the atmosphere of the world that our 'oracle seismographs' have picked up on. I believe that it is both of you, not one, because we have been noticing quite distinct ripples of activity in our graphs, indicating the movement of not one, but two different types of elemental activity. It is highly unlikely, but I suppose that only one of you could possess command of both gifts that we're seeking out. That does happen very rarely, but it is far more likely that you both were unknowingly practicing one type. Seeing the two of you, and the depth of your friendship, further assures me of this; you unconsciously found each other and remain in such close contact one with another because in the far reaches of your souls you recognize similar gifts in the other person, gifts that other people do not possess.

Still unable to comprehend this seemingly fantastic scenario, practical Mignonne attempted, but did not quite succeed, at sarcastically saying, "Okie dokie, Good Sir Omage, how the heck do you plan on us finding out if your 'theory' about us is correct? Personally, I do not intend to stick around here, and you were correct in assuming that we will not go all the way to Africa, so what exactly is your plan?" Mignonne tried to give Omage the stink eye with this remark, but he didn't appear to be dissuaded in any way. But with a disarming calm addressed both girls, "Oh, I know that you're both eager to return to your homes, particularly since I am so assuredly ruffling both your feathers, but there is quite a simple way in order for you and I to discern whether or not I am correct." At this, Omage reached into his cardigan jacket, which didn't exactly match his differently colored dress pants, and pulled out a small bottle. "This liquid is a draft which is designed to be used when ascertaining who true oracles are, and it has been crafted by our people over the years to be used in reliable trial for this reason. Simply take a swallow, it does not have to be a large swallow, and if you truly are an oracle then it will be made known to you. Don't worry, we the Elders have tried to craft this drink to taste quite pleasant as it is going down, and if there you are not an oracle it will not harm you to take it. At worst, you will experience an unpleasant 24-hour stomach bug. We have attempted to use much of the proven scientific theory in our trial and errors trials in making this. Fortunately for you, the Elders were able to sufficiently sculpt a reliable working model years ago." Omage's expression as he said this was the same look that a patient parent uses when they try to convince a small child to take their medicine, but somehow neither Kitty nor Mignonne was reassuringly convinced. They both recognized this expression after innumerable childhood years of their parents trying to persuade them to willingly ingest any kind of cold medicine (Mucinex, or worse, Vick's Nyquil). The girls simply stared at Omage as if to ask if he was seriously asking them to take unlabeled medication off an almost complete stranger; they weren't five, after all. Seeing their reluctance, Omage sighed and pressed the little bottle into Mignonne's hand. "It is alright if the two of you are hesitant. I would expect no less from two of the oracles. We can part ways now, and I will give the two of you time to consider all of this. If you do decide to try this physic (he smiled a little sardonically at this statement), I would recommend doing it when you two are alone in your room, not out per se. It does lead to some occurrences which the general public would see as strange. I will be in contact with the two of you." Mignonne was strongly reminded of Shakespeare's words in *The Tempest*, as Omage did seem to vanish strangely, tossing his rather long dark hair and not really disappearing but leaving the garden so quickly that you could have easily missed it. Sharing a baffled look, the girls stood and started walking (stumbling a little bit; they were rather confused still) back the short distance to the castle/hotel, not even speaking until they were securely back in their tower room.

Not really sure where to begin, Mignonne looked at Kitty and spread her hands out helplessly in front of her, while shaking her head to communicate that she really didn't understand anything that was going on, but eventually she was the first to speak. "Kitty," she said softly, "I'm not exactly sure what to do. Everything that Omage told us sounds bogus and far-fetched, and I'm not sure what a valid thing to do would be... after all, nothing that he said makes any kind of sense, and we've been taught all our lives not to consume anything given by strangers; it could be a date rape drug!" While she saw the logic in what Mignonne was saying, Kitty did have a somewhat different perspective on the whole thing. Kitty stammered and tried to maintain a level voice as she said, "True, but why would he send us alone back to take it if it was a date rape drug. I mean, I know that he's pretty aware of where we're staying and how to get to us if need be, but still doesn't make sense to me." At this point both Kitty and Mignonne shook their heads at stared pointedly at the little bottle lying on their table, guarding themselves as if it were likely to lunge at them and attack. Unable to think of another thing to do, Mignonne finally looked at Kitty in a lost way, saying, "Well, there's no point in standing here staring at it. Let's go grab some lunch at the café that I saw while we were out and think about something else for at least an hour." Kitty happily agreed to this idea, and once the girls had gone down the street and were seated in the tiny restaurant, she was extra pleased to discover that any meal would be billed to their room charge at their hotel somehow (which they weren't paying!). Apparently, the café and the hotel had some kind of a weird understanding. Emboldened by their liking of the porridge that morning, they were both more easily willing to try some true Scottish fare, rather than the more familiar American food. Mignonne decided on traditional Scottish Cock-a-leekie soup (which tasted oddly familiar to American chicken soup, just with more vegetables), while Kitty favored the more vegetarian dish of rumbledethumps, which turned out to be a sort of casserole containing onions, potatoes, and cabbage. Telling each other that their first time in a foreign country warranted a celebration, both young ladies ordered the raspberry cranachan for dessert, and successfully managed to ensure that they stayed happily distracted and were able to speculate in an off-hand way if the Scots put liquor in *everything*, geez.

Chapter 6

Meeting Your Conclusion

After about two hours, Mignonne and Kitty were unable to come up with any further distractions to be had at the café, and so slowly and somewhat reluctantly the girls made their way back to the manor where they staying and up the medieval looking stairs and into their hotel room. Feeling very chill after her big and tasty late lunch, Mignonne sat down in one of the arm chairs near a tiny window, closed her eyes, and then breathed out and made eye contact with Kitty. "Okay KitKat… we've wasted enough time trying to figure out if we should take this liquid or not. How about we take it one at a time so that there's always somebody who's hopefully rational to look out for the other person? Do you think that would work?" Kitty gratefully kept Mignonne's expression, breathing out in gratitude that somebody had managed to come to what seemed like a somewhat legit conclusion. And not knowing what to say at this point, she simply nodded. Mignonne looked at the vial nervously but finally made her decision, and exclaiming kinda breathlessly, "Here goes," just took the bottle and knocked it back into her mouth. The liquid didn't taste bad and was actually quite pleasant after she took a second and thought about what exactly it tasted like. It reminded her of a weird combination of coffee and fruit smoothie, but she couldn't really pinpoint what fruit she was tasting. Maybe guava? Mignonne had only had guava once or twice in her life, and not recently, so she was only vaguely able to remember what it tasted like. As she was sitting in her chair, with Kitty perched on one of the beds and nervously eyeing her in case of an impending nervous snap, Mignonne started noticing only a little increase in the air around her circulating as it picked up speed slightly. As it continued to pick up speed and it became chillier and chillier, she shuddered against it. The wind got strong enough to be really apparent in the room and it knocked a decorative figurine of an intrepid Scotsman off one of bureau tops and it ruffled the edges of the fluffy pillowcases. Before Mignonne or Kitty could get really nervous though, that was the extent of what happened. After her heart rate slowed back down and the random wind stopped, Mignonne exhaled loudly in relief, quickly doing a spot check of her body. Turning to Kitty she passed over the vial. "I guess that's it, Kitty-Me-Dear; I feel fine, and unless I look more weird to you, I think you're safe to take this."

Blinking at the bottle, which was now in her hand, Kitty looked apprehensively at Mignonne. Kitty was actually felt her nerves colliding with each other rapidly and looked with frightened eyes at Mignonne. "How'd you manage to take this, Miggy!? I'm so jangled up! I don't know if I can do this, I'm not as brave as you!" Mignonne had had this conversation with Kitty frequently in all the years that they had known each other and sighed a little as she tried to say softly and with patience, "Don't worry about having bravery, Kitty. I'm not any braver than you, I just got tired of teetering in limbo over a decision and ultimately figured 'oh screw it.' This is a safe zone, so I thought that this was probably the best circumstances that I would find to take this stuff." Looking at Mignonne at little disbelievingly, Kitty closed her eyes and brought the bottle to her lips. She was unable to throw it back with the gusto that she had seen Mignonne do, and she slowly, carefully, tipped the vial over her bottom lip and let the liquid progress with moderation into her mouth and down her throat. Kitty felt really happy that the stuff didn't taste nasty, at least, although the coffee taste was pretty gross to her because of personal tastes with regards to the popular drink. Shuddering a little because of the taste, Kitty put the bottle down on the table and looked up; unless she was very mistaken, the potted plant in the corner was moving upwards, growing bigger but at a rapidly accelerated rate, with the buds that were on the plant (Kitty guessed it was some sort of hibiscus) each bursting open, one after another in quick succession. The potted plant went from just being a tall green stalk about a foot tall to being a fully mature hibiscus plant, with flowers that had gone from nothing to full bloom in a matter of seconds. Kitty actually jumped back a little from the plant, even though it was on the other side of the room, looking back and forth from the plant to Mignonne nervously. "What the hell was that all about!?" Kitty sputtered vigorously, so freaked out by what happened that she used profane language, something that she very rarely did. Wide-eyed, with her gaze also fixed on the plant that had just undergone a tremendous growth spurt, Mignonne shook her head, slowly managing to breathe out her words one at a time. And saying with a muted tone, "I have no frickin idea, Kitty. I don't understand anything that just happened, or what the hell could be in this drink." Doing what she normally did when really nervous, Mignonne proposed that they get in their beds and go to sleep, and maybe this would all go away from their minds. After all, it's not like any of this stuff could actually have *happened*. The drink that Omage had given to them most likely had some strong hallucinogenic properties, they concluded, and hopefully it wouldn't have any long-term ramifications. Climbing into their beds without a further word, Kitty and Mignonne happily surrendered themselves to the oblivion of sleep. Unfortunately, the escape that they sought was not easily found, and though they fell asleep pretty quickly their minds were filled with bizarre dreams all night, dreams that felt closely akin to the hallucinations that they were sure produced the effects that they had seen in the room.

Kitty was startled awake the next morning by the ringing of the hotel phone (how weird that this medieval castle-hotel had phones in the rooms) and with a mind still clouded with sleep groggily answered it. "Yeah…" Kitty managed to rasp out, still not quite able to shake the sleep out of her voice… "So" a familiar male voice answered, "I see that the two of you took the liquid. I must commend you both for partaking with such vigor and rapidity. I will be at the hotel shortly so that I may speak with you both about what happened and what it means, for you two and for the ultimate end goal of the world. I expect that I shall arrive in about ten minutes," Omage said and then hung up. "Miggy, we have to get up; the king of weird is coming soon," Kitty exclaimed as she lurched up and out of bed; stopping on her way to the bathroom to hit the still prostrate Mignonne with a pillow. Kitty raced into the bathroom and began her morning cleanliness rituals. Still in the bathroom brushing her teeth in what she guessed was about five minutes, Kitty was interrupted by Mignonne's voracious rapping at the bathroom door and asking for admission. Spitting toothpaste and water into the sink, Kitty stepped out of the little bathroom so that Mignonne could use the toilet and she started rummaging through her suitcase. Thanking the power that is that she only had about two outfits left to choose from, Kitty put on a casual sundress and slipped into her sandals. She'd intended before to wear this outfit if they ever went out dinner, but she felt that it was appropriate today somehow. Once Mignonne was also sufficiently brushed and dressed (her in jean shorts and light blouse), the two girls headed downstairs, figuring that they would wait for Omage in the lobby, answering an unspoken desire that they both had to keep him away from their hotel room. Mignonne felt like they had barely got downstairs before the front swivel door moved and suddenly Omage appeared inside. He was wearing something today that was even more strange, with a tunic-esque shirt and pants that were not as casual as sweatpants but that were quite obviously made of a different cloth than slacks; they appeared to be too soft to be regular pants. Noticing the two girls staring at him as he came in, Omage smiled more openly than Kitty or Mignonne had seen and quickly crossed the floor to them. They had stood as Omage approached and he clasped each of their hands in turn, having the same expression that a kid has on Christmas morning, almost skipping in place with glee.

"Kitty. Mignonne," Omage began formally, "I am most pleased that the two of you ingested the serum, didn't I tell you that there was no harm in it? If regular people take the serum, after all, nothing happens, it just might taste a little off to them. I am also pleased to inform the two of you that it is as I suspected; you both contain pathways and routes in your bodies which are indicative of the people that the Elders are always seeking." Seeing their confusion and, even with supposed evidence, lots of skepticism, Omage pulled himself into a regal stance and said with authority (where from?), "If you two will accompany me outside into the garden area that is on this site, I will happily tell you both what I mean." Without further ado, Omage walked out the spinning door again, as if feeling totally confident that Mignonne and Kitty would follow him. And since they were now quite ablaze with curiosity, the girls did in fact stand and walk after him, though they did not bother to rush as he seemed to be doing. Having the reached the little garden that the two had been in, seemingly eons ago, Kitty and Mignonne joined Omage, who was standing and looking with what appeared to be some sort of longing into a tiny but still burbling brook. After he stepped away from the edge of the water, Omage threw his shoulders back and faced the two of them, taking his time but finally beginning with the statement, "So. If you two are more open to listening to what I have to say today, please sit down, or remain standing if you would prefer, it makes no difference how you are situated if you two actually *listen* to what I have to say." Exchanging a glance, the girls staunchly remained in an upright position, the better to make their escape should it be necessary. Seeing this, Omage began pacing along the brook and he stared into the distance as he began.

"Life flows at differing paces for each of us, with every person experiencing and comprehending reality at their own rate; every individual in this world is given a particular role that they alone can best fill. This assignment, so to speak, is given to them by the Almighty creator of the universe, and it is the understanding of the Elders that this designation is decided before the person comes into being within the realm of physical reality. Every single person has their own kind of distinction and gifts, but it is quite obvious I'm sure to you two and to others that some roles carry more importance when regarding the overall state of this world. These people make discoveries or serve purposes that affect the entirety of this human existence. Mahatma Gandhi guiding the country of India to a successful adaptation after the people's departure from the caste system is one; the Reverend Dr. Martin Luther King Jr. is another with the civil rights changes which he initiated. Now, I am not in any way making the statement that the importance of the two of you are on par with these men; each life and the actions thereof are judged individually and each of us are examined as to the completion of our own destinies. I only bring up these men who affected the world so positively in order to give a good example of the differing degrees to which a person's life may affect others." Kitty and Mignonne were able to do nothing except stare at Omage, wishing he'd come to any point that particularly addressed them. Seeing their continued attention, Omage proceeded with apparent relief, "After the fall of humankind away from close contact with divinity, even the divine spirits (your people know them as angels) and the facets governing all aspects of human life were affected, with those with malicious intent working without rest or fail on ordering human life negatively. Anything that can be manipulated, people or natural properties, is subject to be changed for the worst under these potentially disastrous directives which are now present in this world. Seeing the existence of this tendency, Yahweh named five people to be in charge some of the most important elements in this battle for the good. These people might or might not be in existence, depending on the needs of any given generation, and they are rarely found in close contact one with another. Because of this, you can imagine the Elders' delight when we discovered that you two were so close in contact and relationship with one another! You two, who are each part of the five that will exist for this time."

Omage did not say all of this without pausing occasionally, looking at the girls as if to gage their reactions; he only continued on if he saw some level of understanding in their faces. Seeming to find confidence as he went on, Omage breathed out and began again. "Your silence so far shows wisdom. Often it is better to wait and absorb information before questions are asked. This part of our discussion will concern each of you individually, though it will be best if you both stay present and attentive while I'm talking, so that you may truly be able to assist one another should the need arise." Omage gave a small, amused half smile as he added, "To create a jumping off point that seems more grounded and stable to the two of you, we will begin with a discussion of Kitty Mun-Stone. You have no idea how appropriate that last name is in relation to who you are. You, Kitty, are the oracle of growth, change, and development in the natural world as it relates to the element of the *terra firma*, the ground and all that grows from it, that provides both nourishment and poison, shade and striking disease and irritation. You have a connection to this element of reality in a way that allows you to guide and control the growth of plants, both those with positive attributes and those with negative, and to use this component both to the greater good and to the potential detriment of humankind. Theoretically, once you have mastered your gift it could be used to help crops of food to grow successfully, or it could be used to promote the potential growth of weeds and poisonous plants, which could lead to the entire downfall of a branch of civilization. Of course, your gift, like all the others, works in balance with the other elements and is unable to do either of these things without the support and presence of the other gifts. I believe that you, Kitty, have your own small garden?"

Kitty's mind, up to this point, had been spinning out of control, but when she realized that Omage was asking her a direct question she attempted to pull herself back together; "Yeah… I guess it is small." Kitty seemed quite miffed when she heard her pride and joy described in a way that she saw as trivializing, and she huffed and her eyes narrowed as she made this remark. Once again smiling in a way that seemed to Kitty to appear weirdly triumphant, Omage's next bit of commentary began. "You have a garden, then, and am I correct in thinking that it is largely successful is the production of vegetables or flowers? It would be my wager that only this garden is a place that you feel very at home in, and that being in it can calm you down when it appears that nothing else can?" Kitty nodded almost imperceptibly, and Omage continued. "This then is in keeping with the traits of the oracle who watches over the soil and the development of growth in it. I will tell you in a brief bit of time how we will proceed with managing this gift." Tired of being confused, Mignonne broke in and came close to yelling when she said, "*We?* What is this '*we*' that you presumptuously say, and why does Kitty, who's supposedly a really, *really* special person, need the help of this alleged **we**?" Omage infuriatingly just smiled again and said, "All will be explained in good time, my dear Ms. Johansen… you have my word on this. This does lead us quite nicely into our next point of discussion before we reach any type of conclusion. If you're feeling quite comfortable so far, Ms. Mun-Stone, we will proceed onto a brief description of Ms. Johansen's gift?" Not waiting for a reply, Omage turned to Mignonne.

Omage seemed less relaxed to be talking to Mignonne now, probably because she kept stating everything that she was thinking, and he quite possibly found this to be pretty rude. Mignonne felt a little pleased that he felt this discomfort when talking to her. It gave her some feeling of power and control in the situation, whether a real power or not. She wasn't sure if Omage knew about this somehow, but it still made her more relaxed. Finally resigning himself, Omage began, "Ms. Johansen; your element is so far apart from Ms. Mun-Stone's that it is not possible to create a further separation. Perhaps this is why the two of you have such an enduring friendship and camaraderie; isn't a common expression in this country that 'opposites attract?' The element over which you have some measure of control and manipulation is the very air that is over the earth. The air that is the figurative life-blood of almost all reality, since there are few things which can exist without the air and the wind. You control the air which contributes to giving the growth of Ms. Mun-Stone's plants, the air that immediately produces alarm and panic when it is denied to people or animals. Air gives life just as firmly as do the plants that nourish our bodies, and it fills an integral role in the ongoing dance that is life. This air can continue life, as it does when it is used in the Heimlich maneuver or even if the everyday breath that we take for granted. But air can also form forces which can stir and manipulate the earth, the water, and fire, as is seen in earthquakes, tsunamis, or wildfires. People do not normally think of air as dangerous, but believe you me, it can be. You, also, will need to learn to manage this gift, and develop ways in which to do this that work for you. And now, young ladies, we have reached the portion of our discussion in which I am waiting, ready and willing, to answer your questions."

The rational mind of Mignonne rebelled against everything that Omage was saying, but in the end she had to admit that it made a lot of sense in some strange way. A sense of peace filled her after Omage finished talking, in spite of the absolute craziness of what the subject was. She could no more explain this chilled out feeling any more than she could explain the feeling of gratitude and relief that you might feel after you made yourself say a hard truth, something that you had been dreading saying. Kitty likewise was experiencing this peace, but her feelings were almost bordering on an inexplicable joy, joy in making a discovery that seemed to answer questions that she did not know that she had, that spoke to her beyond her levels of consciousness and into deeper, more primordial levels. Perhaps more spiritual levels? Kitty didn't know, but she was very thankful for these new and happy mentalities. Kitty almost breathed out in relief once Omage had stopped talking and looked at them; Omage looked at Mignonne and Kitty as if with eager anticipation of their questions. Mignonne finally leveled her gaze with that of Omage and narrowed her eyes. Deciding that it was better to get started quickly and without fear, Mignonne tried to be flippant and casual as she asked, "Okay. So I guess there's a lot that we'll need to figure out with this, but the bigger question, maybe the biggest question and the most pertinent to us, is what do we do now?" This almost came out sounding like a challenge, but Mignonne honestly didn't know of anything else to ask, she was so confused and overwhelmed by everything. "Again, good question, Ms. Johansen," said Omage, who seemed to have switched to addressing the girls more formally after his huge revelation about their identities. "I will tell you what the usual plan is and then we can proceed."

Chapter 7

After High School Plans

"My order of the Elders has attempted to wait until the two of you have reached an age which your culture deems to be adulthood. We did not want to try and begin your developmental training until you both were free within your society to become independent, and so we timed my letter to Ms. Mun-Stone to coincide precisely with your emancipation from the public school system, as important and venerable as that might be." Omage seemed to be trying to look very serious about his statement, but something about his expression made Kitty question his sincerity. "We wanted the two of you to be able to choose how your training would commence, having gained independence from all required engagements in your society. I was sent to meet with the two of you together because since you two already have such a close acquaintance it did not make sense to speak to you separately. I was very pleased to be selected as the one who would come to you two and divulge all of this monumentally important information. The Elders locate the oracles using a method that I suppose you could call what our 'monastery' uses in a way that might be comparable to electronic GPS devices? Although our own devices are much more ancient in origin than anything that the electronic media could come up with, these trackers, so to speak, send us frequencies and the presence of your particular, unique type of 'seismic activity,' and three more of my compatriots in the Elder order have been sent in order to locate and divulge the same information to the other three oracles. Fortunately, one of the others actually has a brother whose location we are aware of, and he will be of much help to us in our search for his brother. Half-brother, but brother nonetheless. I only hope that the one brother is able to locate the other, as this oracle is quite adept at circum-navigating the globe and he never stays in any one place for an extended period of time. The other two should not be too difficult to find, as one of the others is also located in the U.S.A. as you two were, and the last is in Europe just as we are, though he is in England.

"It is the desire of the Elders that the oracles of this generation become closely acquainted as you all are learning to utilize your gifts. If the five of you could form some sort of mutual friendship that would be ideal. Your abilities can be quite dangerous if they are not used correctly and becoming in sync with your fellow oracles will pro-vide an easier way for all of you to learn how to use your gifts. This is much like any large and organized institution; a business, for example, won't function as well as possible if all of the members are not aware of each other and working as one towards a common goal, whatever that might be". Omage paused for a breath here, and Mignonne found that she was only barely still hanging on in this conversation, with her mind deciding of its own accord to stop retaining information; every-thing sounded so insane and bizarre. She did find it interesting that Omage had managed to deliver this spiel without pausing or visibly breathing, though; Mignonne felt sure that he had been breathing, just in breaths too small for her to see. After all, even with all of the weirdness he was spouting she was pretty positive that talking still re-quired a certain amount of oxygen, even for him. Mignonne at-tempted to organize her mind and refocus her attention to the matters that apparently were at hand.

Kitty was having a different experience listening to Omage than Mignonne was; yes, she had felt blindsided at the very beginning, but it somehow was getting less strange the further along she went trying to listen and wrap her mind around what he was saying. Kitty simply logged this new data away in the portion of her brain that she had set aside long ago to enable her to listen and effectively respond to Joanna Stone's out-there psychobabble about everything. It was a little bit more difficult, though, to keep in mind that this was not her mother talking and that she might actually need to use this information to be used again shortly in the conversation, should Omage pause long enough for her and Mignonne to ask any more questions. So far though, the part of her brain that was wrestling with this new bunch of what she kept labeling as *stories* in her mind, was unable to translate anything that she heard into her thinking of cold hard fact. Much as she did with her mother, Kitty unconsciously had decided to use the method of humoring the other person and pretending to understand; *Okay, Omage, that's nice. Would you like a cup of herbal tea?* This isn't to say that Kitty thought all of Joanna's stories and theories were not valid, she just had long since learned to deflect her mother from a tirade so that she could have time to think how to respond. As confident as she might be in these abilities though, Kitty was pulled up short with Omage's next statement, and she was too stunned to know how to immediately reply.

Omage settled back into his chair and leaned forward, as if to make sure that neither girl missed any of his next utterance; apparently this was something that he'd had to warm himself up to passing along, though Kitty couldn't see how this might be any more strange than anything that he'd said before. "So, Kitty, Mignonne," Omage paused again and took a deep intake of breath, "I have tried to explain in a small way the importance of you two coming to know the other oracles; may I assume that the two of you are aware of the concept of *roommates*, in an academic or social setting? Say, in the habitat of a university?" Kitty looked at Mignonne with a bewildered expression, trying to communicate the question *what the hell is this guy talking about? Of course, we know how college works,* without speaking a word. Mignonne met Kitty's eyes and looked just as confused as she did so. "Very good," Omage continued, either missing or choosing not to see Mignonne and Kitty's expressions, "I know that this may seem to be quite a stretch for the of you, but perhaps you would be willing to consider relocating? We won't ask you to move anywhere very strange, only somewhere located on the moors of Scotland?" Omage smiled hopefully after he said this. "This is part of the reason why I wanted to have the two of you meet me here; so that you might acquaint yourselves with this place, therefore feeling less upheaval when you move here? The Elders have purchased a home for the oracles located on the edge of Edinburgh, and it is our wish that all of the oracles occupy this space, for a time at least. Being located here will put everyone in close proximity to the seat of King Arthur, who I'm certain you're aware of from British lore? This is a place steeped in the history and, for lack of a better word, the *magic* of ancient Europe, and the Elders feel that this place will be highly conducive to all of the oracles effectively learning to use their skills.

"Okay, stop me if I'm incorrect," Mignonne began following what she saw as an absurd proposition, "You want me and Kitty to move here? So that we can occupy a house with three total strangers? That doesn't sound like a bad idea *at all.*" Mignonne was really unable to keep talking after this, finding herself tongue tied and her head spinning. Seeing that her friend had checked out mentally, Kitty sprung into the conversation with her own summary of events. "Okay, so practically speaking, when would we need to do this? We've got a lot to do back home if this happens, like we need to update our medical records, convince our parents to let us do this, and pack our stuff. Oh, and there's that slight matter of *convincing ourselves that you're not a raving lunatic!*" After this pronouncement both Kitty and Mignonne jumped out their seats once Kitty exploded with this accusation, but to their utter surprise Omage threw his head back and *laughed!* Wiping the tears of laughter out of the corner of his eyes, Omage continued to smile as he said with quite obvious relief, "Ladies, ladies... I would expect nothing less from two of the oracles! Of course, you're worried about all of these trivial details! Not the least of which is your relational itinerary with you families while doing this! I don't need any confirmation about anything today, tomorrow, or even this week. Of course it'll take a little time for the two of you to believe and trust me. After all, what I've just told the two of you I'm sure sounds quite preposterous, not lending much credibility to my own sanity. That being said, I will leave you ladies to mull everything over, considering your identities and what this could mean in relation to your lives. However, I will need an affirmative response from one or both of you before the end of summer. The current Elders have never had any group of oracles to deal with, and so we are a little lost as to how best to work with all of you in the modern world. We would like this response in good time so that we may confirm with the other Elders who are presently seeking out the other oracles and we will try and come up with a valid time frame in which everything may conceivably happen."

Omage stood up after this and pulled a few sheets of paper out of his chic but severely mismatched blazer. "Here are return plane tickets for the two of you, along with information about how to call for taxi services to get you to the airport. If you'll note, the tickets are for two days from now. I thought this best in order to give you time to process all of the information that I've shared with you whilst hopefully being away from most distractions. I have included a telephone number as well with these tickets. This is a number that will reach me directly, going to a cellular telephone that I purchased for this exact purpose." Omage smiled knowingly after he said this, which kind of pissed Mignonne off, though she wasn't entirely sure why. He passed the tickets and the other papers to Kitty, nodded at the girls, and without another word gracefully took his leave from the garden. Mignonne found herself still really frustrated with the ease that he disappeared with; she wondered whether his seeming disappearances came from learned traits or if they were common to his culture, maybe? Kitty looked at Mignonne with panicked eyes while Mignonne was having these ruminations, and she swallowed and managed to speak, though her voice trembled. "Miggy, maybe we could go sit down somewhere and just talk a little about what all this could mean? I mean, I just think that I'll able to handle this better if we talk and really hash this out." "Okay, Kit-Kat, we can do that. How 'bout we stay outside and sit back down on these benches and talk?" Mignonne knew that Kitty would feel more relaxed in an outdoor setting, and she was seriously afraid that Kitty, or perhaps she herself, was about to snap. She figured that maybe if Kitty felt better, she'd feel better. "We can just stay in the garden and talk about what this means. Seriously, I thought getting accepted into college was going to be the weirdest thing that we'd have to decide after high school, but apparently not," she added using a sing song voice, trying to lighten the mood.

Kitty seated herself in the garden and tried to do what Joanna was always going on about and center herself; she closed her eyes, took slow, deep breaths, and tried to keep herself calm and thinking rationally about everything. After only a few minutes Kitty felt a little better and opened her eyes to look at the worried face of Mignonne. "First order of business for the discussion of this life-changing, absolutely insane idea: Do we believe Omage?" Feeling relieved that Kitty had actually launched the topic, Mignonne shook her head and breathed out "I don't know; it seems a little stupid weird to believe him, but stuff did happen after we took the serum-stuff. And he did correctly talk about our lives and interests, but I don't know... what do you think we could do so we could know for sure?" Kitty got frustrated all over again listening to this non-answer; why couldn't Mignonne have done more than just naming the stuff that they knew?! I mean, yes, Omage did know some interesting stuff about them, and they had reacted to the serum, but what if this liquid was designed to react in similar ways to everyone? What if Omage was trying to sucker them into some kind of huge human trafficking scenario? Okay, yes, he had obviously gone to great lengths with money and time to get them here and talk to them, but how could they be sure that this wasn't an elaborate front?

While she was pondering these things, Kitty's eyes drifted down and she suddenly decided to examine the so-called "plane tickets" that Omage had given them today. Upon examination the tickets *looked* legit, with the symbol for Scottish Air and a specific departure time and date (in two days at 10:00 A.M.), and the car service detail page also looked real, naming a popular cab service, but who really, *really* knew for goodness' sake? Mignonne decided to check and double check the online details about the tickets and the cab service on a computer in the manor lobby, and both checked out as real stuff that other people were using daily. Mignonne breathed a relieved 'phew' once this was discovered and began to start to seriously wonder if Omage might be telling them the truth. I mean, stranger things happened all the time, right? Mignonne showed Kitty the website for the airline and gave her a relieved smile; after all, what kind of sex-crazed psychopath sent his victims home to think about it? She matter-of-factly stated, "I vote we go home, pack, and prepare for a really, really, really big adventure! Who knew we would get the chance for all this cool and weird stuff to do right after high school?!" After she said this, Mignonne jumped to her feet and motioned for Kitty to follow her back into the room. Kitty was not as immediately excited about all this as Mignonne was, but she too was tremendously relieved (even if the relief was just to be going home) and shaking her head she followed Mignonne back up the stairs to begin trying to reassemble the Ecu-Nu travel bag that Joanna had been so excited to get for her for her trip.

Chapter 8

Decisions

Mignonne and Kitty really didn't feel up to talking much once they exited the plane at the airport back home in the U.S. Getting up early to finish packing after not sleeping really well the night before and then being unable to eat breakfast because she was too keyed up didn't set a good precedent for Mignonne's day of travel. Kitty also wasn't feeling at her best simply because she hated flying; she shared Joanna Stone's disgust at the fuel usage and amount of carbo emissions that they produced. Add to that 7 hours of being on a flight, followed by a serious baggage location issue, and Mignonne and Kitty really didn't feel like talking. The girls hadn't talked on the flight itself because they were squished like sardines in the flight cabin with the other passengers and were a little nervous about sounding like nutcases to random strangers (though in retrospect, neither girl really knew why this was; I mean, it wasn't like they'd ever see these people again, but both girls felt like they'd been given a random secret that had to be kept away from prying eyes and ears). The airport was a madhouse anyway once they got off the plane and retrieving their luggage from the baggage carousels proved to be enough of challenge. It required their full attention and alertness, and Mignonne's toiletries bag still never showed up. Be that as it was, eventually an exhausted Kitty and Mignonne stumbled out into the late afternoon sun and attempted to locate their ride. Clark Johansen had again kindly offered to be of concierge service and pick both girls up at the airport, dropping Kitty off at her house on the way home. Remembering the fiasco that she and her mother had had on the bus trying to make it to the airport, Kitty had gladly accepted his offer, and Clark helped her and Mignonne load their baggage into the blessedly free-of-twins minivan.

Once Clark had handed Kitty and her luggage over to a gushingly grateful Joanna Stone, he and Mignonne drove back to their house, where Sasha and Caleb assaulted Mignonne like she'd been gone for weeks. Finally managing to pry them off, Mignonne waved to her mom and dragged her bag upstairs to her room, using the excuse of travel exhaustion to throw her suitcase onto the floor and fall fully clothed onto the bed, where she sprawled out and let herself really relax for the first time in three days. Her promise to give the twins and her parents a detailed account of the trip at dinner was the only thing that kept them out of her room, and Mignonne was fairly certain that this wouldn't last. True to form, the twins came traipsing into her bedroom after about half an hour, demanding details of her long, long trip and searching her suitcase not really secretly for presents (she had gotten them each a little tourist trinket at the airport in Scotland). Meanwhile, Kitty was enjoying a much quieter time at her home, with Joanna helping her to unpack but not immediately insisting on any kind of details. Kitty was once again thankful that Joanna's constant chattering didn't always require a response. And once she had finished helping Kitty to unload her bags, Joanna hustled to the tiny kitchen to make tea while Kitty prepared herself to give a drawn out account of the trip at any rate. She knew that once the tea was ready, Joanna would be eagerly anticipating this spiel. Not wanting to call each other so immediately following the trip, Kitty and Mignonne each made it through their various family trials, retreated into their bedrooms (Kitty's was little more than a cupboard located off the kitchen), and fell into a restful sleep, thankful to be home and to not have to immediately think of what Omage had proposed for their after high school plans, postponing the decision making until they both felt sufficiently rested.

The sun seemed to emerge far too soon for a still sleepy Kitty, who was surprised at herself. She usually deeply loved rising early and having a few peaceful moments to bask in the rays of a bright sun before the turmoil of the day started. Be that as it may, this morning she didn't feel peaceful or extremely happy, especially when she thought of what she and Mignonne needed to talk about today. Kitty knew that Mignonne wouldn't be up for a few hours at least and would be really cranky-pants if not allowed to have a substantial breakfast before The Talk commenced. That's what Kitty found herself calling it… The Talk. That probably made it feel much more important than she was allowing herself to believe that it was. Yes, it most likely was going to have large bearings on the lives, but really, giving it such precedence gave it too much power in the immediate importance of today. These were the things that Kitty made herself think, and she didn't allow herself to pause and ponder whether or not they were true. Mignonne, likewise, did what she normally did when faced with a talk or a paper that she didn't really want to do. She forced herself to logically think about every detail of what had transpired from a logical standpoint, weighing facts and analyzing data in a succinct and ,yes, logical way. She and Kitty had agreed to meet today at Kitty's house, both of them knowing that is would be more quiet and peaceful than Mignonne's. They could probably manage to have a decent conversation at Kitty's house. At the appointed time, Mignonne set out on the short walk down the road to Kitty's cottage, trying to figure out what she was going to tell Kitty that she thought about everything and what she thought they should do.

Seeing her beloved Miggy walk onto her porch from her vantage point up in a tree, Kitty forced herself to immediately jump down.

"Helloooo, Mignonne! Right here!" she called once she was on the ground below the willow in her garden. Mignonne's immediate reaction was a happy smile when she saw her best friend, but this quickly faded as she and Kitty almost cautiously approached each other, eyeing each other warily as if they each expected the other person to into some kind of random crazed psychopath. That was what this discussion seemed like to them. Stalling, Kitty grinned nervously at Mignonne and used checking her mailbox as an excuse to avoid immediately starting a conversation. Avoiding looking at Mignonne, Kitty pulled a pretty substantial bunch of letters out of the mailbox. Bills, Mother Earth News magazine for Joanna, spam… Kitty didn't think that anything really interesting was present until she sorted through to the bottom of the pile and saw a random packet from the University of Glasgow. Mignonne moved closer to her to look at the envelope and raised questioning eyes to Kitty. Kitty shrugged and opened the letter. She didn't think that she'd *applied* to go to a college anywhere off the continental U.S., but knowing how forgetful she often was, Kitty opened the fairly substantial package and found, lo and behold, an acceptance letter! The package was complete with a packet of courses of study that were offered by the university, and a financial aid document. Before Kitty could get too weirded out, Mignonne pulled another letter from the bottom of the stack, which had been hiding behind the dorm listings page, and Kitty and Mignonne huddled together to read it.

Dear Kitty,

I thought it might be easier for you and Mignonne to communicate your relocation to Scotland to your families if they believed that you were going to be attending one of the prominent universities here. I have attempted to include all of the typical information which is present in an acceptance letter in this packet. I believe that should your parents for any reason examine the seal of the university present on your acceptance letter, for example, they will find it to be identical to the crest of the university. Of course, you might find this to be too presumptuous on my part, but I thought that this might ease your and Mignonne's minds with moving out of the country and starting a new branch of your lives. I am sending you and Mignonne both this imposter acceptance letter and school information, and if you choose to "accept" this opportunity, please send me a response as per U.S.P.S. to the address which is listed in this letter. And I will send you both airline tickets and instructions for disembarkation in Scotland. I wish the two of you all the best, and you have my high hope that you two enjoy a pleasant summer vacation.

Omage, the Order of the Elders, 2020

Finishing up reading and rereading this letter, Kitty and Mignonne looked at each other with bewildered eyes, attempting to grasp at words that would be appropriate and/or make sense after they read Omage's missive. "So," began Mignonne, folding her arms and hugging herself in what was unconsciously a defensive posture, "Omage seems to have gone to a whole bunch of trouble to help us to move to Scotland. We have a valid excuse, and if what Omage says in his letter is true, he'll once again get us plane tickets and probably continue to pay for our stay if it turns out like our *last* trip to Scotland." "Yeah," Kitty murmured, "it seems like he's really kinda desperate to get us there. And if he went to the trouble of sending us fake college acceptance letters, then he plans for us to be there at least for a few years. This is all really weird, and I'm not sure that I like it. I mean, I liked what we saw of Omage, and I liked what we saw of Scotland, but *really*?" Mignonne shook her head and joined in with a very baffled expression, continuing to shake her head and eventually saying, "I know; did you sign up for this weirdness, Kitty? Because I sure didn't".

Mignonne's dialogue continued as she rambled on, also trying to reassure herself. "However, we're young, we're cute, we're not old enough be thinking like older, rational adults of the human species. I mean, when in our placid, complacent lives have we ever had a chance like this? A chance to just say, 'To hell with it,' and go after something, not stopping to think like stupid logical adults. If this turns out to be a mistake, we can just leave and come back to our normal, boring existence." Here Mignonne paused, cocked her head, and smiled mischievously, looking at Kitty with eyes full of excitement. "It doesn't make any kind of sense, but I say let's go for it. What's the worst that could happen? We could get kidnapped and sold to a country that will disapprove of our lifestyles and clothes? If Omage wanted to do that, he could've easily done that the *first* time we met him outside the country. I say let's go, and may the force be with us." Here Mignonne concluded her little rant, breathed out, and looked expectantly at Kitty, hoping to see mutual feelings of excitement.

Kitty didn't see this scenario through Mignonne's rose-colored glasses, and she was really more nervous than excited when she thought about doing what Mignonne was proposing. But as had often happened in their years of friendship, Kitty tried to look at it from Mignonne's perspective and do what would make her friend happy. In the past, this decision had only led to mistakes like getting kicked out of a movie theatre for being too loud or getting caught by a teacher for exchanging notes in class, but *this was big!* Could she treat it the same way, really? Kitty's blood started pounding in her ears and as she sat down on the dirt when her head started spinning; she was surprised to find that when she came back to her senses, she kind of agreed with Mignonne. After all, *who said that she couldn't do something impulsive and possibly stupid?!* Making this decision to walk on the wild side gave Kitty a great sense of hope and expectancy.;Sshe figured that when she was laying on her death bed (hopefully many, many years in the future), she would be happy that she'd took this chance, that she and Mignonne had ventured together into the realms of the unknown. Meeting Mignonne's eyes, Kitty steadied her voice and tried not to jump up and down with joy as her words came tumbling out: "Okay, Miggy. Let's do this thing."

The girls were too excited to wait to respond to Omage's missive, and Kitty accompanied Mignonne back to her house where Mignonne's was temporarily distraught when she checked her own mailbox and discovered nothing in it. Before she could get really worked up though, Mignonne's instincts told her to run inside and check in case somebody else had already gotten the mail. And sure enough, a stack of letters accompanied by a few magazines was sitting on the table in the kitchen that was substantially larger than Kitty's mail stack had been. Mignonne's mother, Emma, was standing in the doorway into the hall when the girls burst in, and she smiled when she saw the supposed acceptance letter to the University of Glasgow in Kitty's hands. "Well, Mignonne. I get the feeling that you and Kitty are both going to want to leave and go frolicking across the ocean for school? It's so great that you both got big 'welcome aboard' letters from Scotland! This will work out great in connection with the two of you doing an internship with Kitty's uncle, which I guess will last longer than the two days that you two were gone this week?" Emma Johansen broke off here, seeming to realize that this might really mean that her babies were really, *really* going away for school. Mignonne watched as this realization dawned on her mother, taking the opportunity to open her own package, finding in it similar school documents as Kitty's, along with a similar but much briefer note from Omage detailing about plane tickets and such. She guessed that Omage really didn't want to entertain the possibility that she and Kitty wouldn't want to take him up on his offer, and that he was really using wishful thinking almost dangerously in writing his letters to the two of them. Mignonne and Kitty both ran forward and hugged Emma after Mignonne got done looking briefly over her letter, both of them feeling a little sad as they listened to Emma's sniffles. Mignonne patted Emma's back consolingly, saying, "It's okay, Mom. Yes, I think we'll be going, but it's not for forever! You can write me or call me anytime! I'll make sure to stay in touch, 'cause I'll miss you and Dad, and I wouldn't want to miss hearing about any of Sasha and Caleb's shenanigans!" Seeing that her mother wasn't really consoled yet, Mignonne shot her a saucy grin as she added, "Besides... I'll need to make sure that you and Dad haven't been admitted into an insane asylum dealing with them and I come and spring you out." At this statement Emma started giggling through her tears and was soon rocking with desperate laughter, holding the girls and alternately laughing and crying. Eventually Kitty and Mignonne got away upstairs into Mignonne's room, where they had their own laughter and tears, refusing to think of any negative possibilities that might come of this, and preparing to really enjoy their last summer at home for a little while.

A crash is inevitable following any super-keyed up time of euphoria. Kitty and Mignonne were young so while upstairs at the home of the Johansen's their state of stupid happy lasted a very short period of time before reality came crashing in as Mignonne sat at her desk and started to compose an affirmative response letter to Omage. What on earth should she say in response to this letter? That yes, they were throwing caution to the wind, venturing forth into the great unknown of young adulthood? How should she phrase that? And speaking of that, when should she and Kitty say they would want to come out, since Omage had asked for this information in his own letter? Eventually Mignonne got tired of sitting paralyzed at her desk and staring blankly at the paper that seemed determined not to be filled. She flung her pen down and tipped back in her chair, holding herself in a precarious position of barely holding onto gravity. "Kitty!" she whined, "Are we really going to be this nuts and do this? Gahhhh!" Fortunately, or maybe not so fortunately, one of Kitty's mantra's in life was to stick to decisions once they had been made, so she felt nothing but a nonsensical high when she contemplated her and Mignonne's decision. Kitty grabbed the pen from Mignonne's hand and leaned over the desk, huffing and puffing as she bent down to scribble the letter herself. "What's the matter, Miggy? You were so brave about this whole thing this afternoon! Now is no time to wuss out! *I'll* write to Omage!" The reply that was composed by Kitty eventually stated this:

Dear Omage (and the Elders?),

Mignonne and I have decided to accept your kooky invitation and move (at least temporarily), to Scotland to work with you. This is our free-will choice, and if we should ever want to come home, we will do that. We will tell our parents the general area that we'll be in, so if you guys decide to keep us for ransom or something, they'll get pretty worried if they don't regularly hear from us or we don't sound happy when we communicate, and they'll be able to alert local authorities if needed. Anyways, we would like to come out close to September? That would make sense if we're pretending to go to school in Scotland. So, I guess that's all my dear pretend relative; we'll hear from you soon.

Kitty and Mignonne

Once Mignonne had retrieved postage stamps and an envelope from her parents' home office, the girls addressed the letter to the address that Omage had provided on his own missive, and they ran outside to put the letter into the mailbox for next day pickup from the postal service. This felt a lot like a final decision had been made to Mignonne and Kitty, and although Mignonne was still a little nervous, she shook her head and supposed that they would have to follow through now. Kitty returned to her tiny house, and Mignonne got ready for bed in her comfortably normal bedroom and bathroom, taking comfort in the normalcy of sorting through the hamper for her pajamas and trying not to dwell too much on coming events. And so Kitty and Mignonne slept, pretty peacefully, though awakening with trepidation the next day to memories of their decisive, and quite possibly reckless, action.

Chapter 9

Final Boarding Call

Mignonne and Kitty's last few months at home were not really peaceful, but then, they never were when you were dogged constantly by rampant, much younger siblings, either yours or your best friend's. Caleb and Sasha both viewed Kitty as an extension of their big sister. She'd been around since they were born, after all, and probably was there beforehand for a little while they guessed. As their assumed older sister, the twins treated Kitty much the same way that they treated Mignonne, feeling that her continued and constant presence in their lives warranted they give to her the same treatment that their older, and in their eyes, venerable big sister got. Because of this, they felt free to subject Kitty and Kitty's house/bedroom to the same ministrations with which they treated Mignonne's, ravaging her stuff, unpacking and looking through her travel bags, and generally making a nuisance of themselves with their constant questions which they viewed to have vital importance. Where you going? Why? What you gonna do there? Why? How you gonna get there? Why? Because of this, both Kitty and Mignonne were very ready to use the airlines tickets which Omage had sent to them a mere week after their reply. Granted, the tickets were for September 3 and it was May, so they unfortunately had a long wait before they left and were forced to pack in secret to try and avoid the constant appraisal of Sasha and Caleb. The Johansen's had told Caleb and Sasha that this year Mignonne was going to be going off to school really far away, and they saw this summer as their last chance to subject her and her friend to their version of tough love.

The weather finally stopped being so stiflingly hot, and Kitty checked and rechecked her baggage repeatedly out of nerves over her impending departure. Kitty even decided to make lists of what she deemed to be necessary accoutrements for personal hygiene, wardrobe, and her own sanity. On top of her earth friendly bathroom supplies lay several CDs of yogic mantras and a handheld player so that she would be able to go in a Zen meditative state if she started freaking out too much at any point. Thinking in a similar way, Mignonne preferred to pack far too many books to distract herself. *Anne of Green Gables* had been a favorite for her while she was young, and she hoped that it would give her the same feeling of escapism now. Escape into a safer, more serene atmosphere. Both girls figured they would probably really need outlets to keep themselves from losing their metaphorical marbles.

While trying to focus on reading her newest book from the library, without much luck, Mignonne heard a soft voice say, "Mignonne." This strangely solemn voice of Mrs. Johansen broke into Mignonne's reverie late one August evening. "I know that you're just about finished getting ready for your and Kitty's flight next week, and I just wanted to check and make sure that you have everything you need." Emma Johansen tried to keep her voice from breaking as she said this, and she looked so close to tears that Mignonne sprang off her floor and threw her arms around her mom. "It's okay, Mom, please don't cry; I bet that Kitty and I will be back before you have time to really miss us." Mignonne tried to speak purely happily as she joked, "Besides, Double and Trouble I'm sure will keep you pretty distracted." This made Mrs. Johansen smile in spite of herself, and she just shook her head and pushed away from Mignonne, escaping into the hallway before anything got really embarrassingly intense since she was not really in touch with her emotions and didn't want to start sobbing. After she left, Mignonne sighed and returned to her book, but she was seized with a sudden burst of excitement that made her reading extremely difficult. She sprawled across her bed and let out a muffled yell into her pillow.

Meanwhile, Kitty was at her house also trying to finish getting prepared to leave. Kitty finally decided that her suitcase would not benefit from any further rechecking, and Kitty forced herself to go leave it alone and go join Mrs. Stone in the small kitchen (besides, if she looked through her clothes anymore Kitty knew that she would have to run them through the washer again, and she really hated doing laundry; plus, they might eventually come to pieces). When Kitty walked into the kitchen, Joanna Stone was sitting at the table, her hands clasped around a mug of herbal tea. "Any tea left, Mom?" Kitty's voice interrupted Joanna's thoughts and startled her into a tiny jump. "Yes, sweetie, there's about half a pot left." Mrs. Stone avoided looking at Kitty as Kitty went and retrieved and filled a mug. Kitty intentionally sat right across from Joanna so she would be forced to look at her. Once eye contact had been established, Kitty said, "Mom. I'm leaving in a couple of days. Are you going to be okay here all alone?" Kitty tried to keep her voice quiet, calm, and reasonable, knowing that Joanna would respond best to this tone. Joanna did eventually break into a smile and even laughed a little as she quietly avowed, "I'll be fine, Kitty. I'm just so excited that you're getting the chance to do this! How many people get this kind of opportunity, especially right out of high school! Plus, you getting a chance to really get to know your biological family is so astounding and wonderful! I'm so thrilled for you!" Joanna broke off here, apparently not trusting her voice to continue. It's not that she didn't mean what she had said, just, she was still sad about everything. However, Joanna Stone was not about to rain on Kitty's parade in any type of way, and she did know how great an opportunity this was for her daughter. "Besides," Joanna continued after a tiny bit, "I'll be so busy with my new chance to work with the local YMCA that I'll be too busy to really notice!" Joanna had been recently offered an opportunity to teach class several times a week at the YMCA on sustainable gardening while watching out for your impact on the environment. Kitty had forgotten about her mom's upcoming teaching gig, and was so relieved to remember. Joanna wouldn't be entirely without human contact when she left at least, and maybe she might make some new like-minded friends. Kitty returned her mom's smile, and she and Mrs. Stone both fell silent with relief and finished their teas.

Like their graduation day, the morning of Kitty and Mignonne's departure dawned cool and bright, as if this part of the world was breathing them a cheerful goodbye. Mignonne got in the family mini-van with both her parents and the twins, who had been come along to say goodbye to their older sister, and who had been threatened with severe punishment by Mrs. Johansen if they didn't maintain at least a little composure. Kitty's mom, not wanting to waste any personal time with her daughter, had declined the Johansens' offer for a ride to the airport, and called a cab to come and pick up her and Kitty (a bus would've been crowded and probably messy, and Joanna Stone didn't want to risk any distractions in what she saw as her last for a while ride with Kitty). Both girls eventually arrived at the airport and with much struggling and help from family got all of their luggage into their terminal. Mignonne was quite nervous as to whether the tickets that Omage had again sent them would work, although she supposed that she probably shouldn't be this nervous. The airline tickets that he'd sent before had worked. She supposed that her nerves were looking for an excuse to be really wired up and maybe were looking for chances to be really wound up that existed apart from the real world.

The tickets did in fact work, and once the boarding call for their flight was announced, the girls each give their own and the other person's parents farewell hugs. And then Mignonne and Kitty each gave a hug to the twins, who seemed to finally realize what was happening, that their sisters were leaving and might not come back for a while, and were mute and non-responsive when Kitty and Mignonne hugged them. Mignonne and Kitty smiled at each other and then got in line to board the plane, each turning at the last moment before they entered to wave one last time at their families. They felt quite the seasoned travelers as they found their seats and settled in for the flight, feeling less fear than eager anticipation for their upcoming adventure. This excitement over a new time in their lives grew as the plane began its assent into the atmosphere, and it held on throughout the flight. The complimentary glass of ginger ale did not hurt this excitement either (Kitty especially was thrilled with this; Joanna didn't allow anything other than water and tea to be consumed in her house). Mignonne finished her drink and then looked out the window at the clouds, getting lost in the intricate shapes and formations, feeling super grateful that she and Kitty had such a long and enduring friendship that they didn't feel the need to fill every moment with idle chatter. Eventually of course, the plane landed in Scotland, and nervousness made the girls suddenly start talking really fast, often overlapping each other's words. Both ladies felt super jumpy as they followed the line of people leaving the plane and stepped into the bright sun of the Scottish day.

Chapter 10
Getting Settled

As Kitty and Mignonne disembarked the plane in Scotland, the first order of business was to try to fight the crowd that was gathering around the slowly revolving baggage claim. The luggage for their flight hadn't appeared yet when they arrived, so they found themselves aimlessly looking around, trying not to stare at people wearing what they assumed was a Scottish attire. It's not that it was so different than what they were used to, just being in an entirely new place once again made them look and see differences in everything. After Mignonne and Kitty successfully claimed their suitcases (which were bigger and more abundant than their previous visit-to-Scotland bags), they walked towards the front doors of the airport. Mignonne was really weighed down by her bags, as she had chosen a long time ago a luggage set that was more pleasing to the eye than practical. She really missed having the little wheels on her suitcases right now. Kitty, whose luggage did have the roller wheels, was more preoccupied with worry about whatever was coming next. Would Omage be there to meet them? Would they go back to the hotel, or somewhere new? How would they get food? Restaurants, or would they be obliged to cook something somehow? She was really hungry. Kitty wondered if Mignonne was having these same thoughts, and then she realized how far ahead of her Mignonne had gotten while she was thinking, and she hurriedly tried to catch up. Mignonne wasn't really caught on thoughts such as these at the moment, as her primary preoccupation was with her feeling like a pack mule as she was so weighed down by her luggage. Sure, on a far-off part of her mind these things might have been occurring to her, but they were not of immediate concern. Her real concern, both of their real concerns, was finding someone, anyone, who knew what was happening next.

Kitty and Mignonne stood with their bags at the entrance of the airport, confusedly looking around to find Omage. Kitty looked at Mignonne and worriedly asked, "You think he'll be here, right? That we didn't miss anything about getting on a bus and going somewhere?" "I really don't think we could've missed anything; the way that I tried to analyze everything before we left so something like this wouldn't happen, I don't think I could've missed any details like that," came Mignonne's response. She really tried to sound nonchalant, but her voicing became a squeak at the end of her speech and gave her away. Mignonne hurriedly blew some hair off her face in what she hoped was a way that disguised her fear. Kitty shifted up and down on her feet, seriously scanning the group of people surrounding them for any signs of anything, *anything*, that explained what was becoming a frightening, awkward situation. Thankfully, while she was making this desperate scan of the room, her gaze lighted on Omage. She would have never believed that she could be so glad to see him and his semi-creepy self, but her slowing heart rate assured her that she was. Omage strode over to the girls, seeming less giddy with excitement than the last time he had seen them, but still appearing pretty pleased. "Kitty, Mignonne, it is so nice to see the two of you. I do apologize for not being present and waiting for your plane as it came in, my order is undergoing an extremely stressful time trying to locate the other oracles and persuade them to come here. You are the only two that as yet we have been successful in getting here." At this point, Omage looked comfortably pleased with himself, apparently attributing the girls successful arrival at least partially to his own powers of persuasion. "If you ladies would be so kind as to accompany me into my vehicle, I shall take the two of you to your new home. Philippe and Adair will attend to your baggage." Was it Mignonne's imagination, or did Omage look slightly less pleased when he looked at the amount of hers? *Oh well,* she thought to herself, *he didn't give us a baggage limit or anything.* Instead of coming to get them in a luxurious town car, this time Omage had come in a what looked like a well-maintained minivan. It seemed he had anticipated the fact that one or both of the girls would come seriously overburdened, even if he didn't like it.

As soon as the luggage was safely packed into the back of the van, Kitty and Mignonne climbed in; Mignonne was so nervous at this point that she nearly threw up out of a nervous response. It wasn't that either of the girls seriously feared that Omage had been running a long con to apprehend them and sell them into slavery or anything, really, but still. Omage seemed disinclined to speak much over the car trip, and the girls were a little apprehensive about discussing their fears in front of him, Philippe, or Adair. First point of making it through a conflict, show no fear, they remembered from watching certain episodes on The Discovery Channel. They still got even more nervous though, as the car made its way past the city which was adjacent to their airport and did not stop anywhere in this somewhat urban area. It meandered, it seemed to Kitty, quite leisurely through the city and entered into a countryside that was so rich and vibrant that she was momentarily distracted in admiring it. Mignonne didn't care as much about the picturesque scene that was passing the car windows, she was too apprehensive and jumpy. She was also kind of chilly, and she assumed that the crazy driver (Philippe or Adair?) had turned on the AC to a ridiculously high level. Her hair was even blowing a little in the breeze generated by it. Mignonne was momentarily distracted with wondering why Kitty's hair or anyone else's for that matter didn't seem to be moving, but this thought was pushed to the back of her mind with the abrupt stopping of the car in front of what looked like a multi-level refurbished farmhouse.

It was a surprising look for a house, even out here on the moors of Scotland, Kitty thought as everyone got out of the car. It looked like in a past life it had been a cottage, but had had much expansion and renovating done on it, and so it was far, far bigger than any cottage that Kitty was familiar with, like her place back home. The main part of the building was kind of a soft cream/not-quite-lemon color, and the shutters and roof a muted brown. Apparently, this cottage had been designed not to attract a great deal of attention from passersby, at least from the colors which were picked, Mignonne thought in spite of her nerves. The colors were so soft and muted, very unassuming, anyway. Omage led the girls up the driveway, which was covered in smooth, highly compacted, grayish-brown peat, and proceeded to unlock the front door. To help relieve the girls' very apparent nervousness, even though it was still early afternoon and quite light outside, Omage flipped on all of the lights as he walked in followed by Kitty, Mignonne, and eventually the two fully laden baggage handlers, Adair and Philippe. "Here we are, ladies," Omage said as he turned to face them in what appeared to be a sparsely furnished living room with a large stone fireplace. The floor was also stone it looked like and was covered in a plethora of mats and rugs so that it wouldn't be too cold to walk on barefoot. "The two of you are free to go into any of the adjoining parts of the cottage once I have left and choose your sleeping chambers. You two will get first choice, as you are the first ones here, but I entreat you, once you have chosen a particular room, remain inhabiting that room for the duration of your stay here, which I hope will be quite long. After all, sticking with our commitments is still an important lesson to learn in life." Omage looked quite lofty and superior as he said this. "Another member of the Elders will return to this cottage in the morning promptly at 9:00 o'clock to bring the two of you to the headquarters of the Elders in Scotland. Once there, we will give you two more information pertaining to what you are to do here in Scotland for your day-to-day life. The refrigerator is fully stocked, should you so desire to cook your supper, and I assure you that the kitchen has been equipped with all of the necessary utensils for doing so." Before Mignonne or Kitty could ask any questions, Omage motioned to Philippe and Adair, and the three of them walked briskly out of the house. Kitty and Mignonne looked at one another in wonderment and shook their heads.

The first order of business once the girls had recovered from the shock of the abrupt nature of their arrival in Scotland was to quickly send "Safely arrived!" text messages to their parents, both cell phones having been equipped to contact other countries before they left the U.S. Once this was completed, the next task, even before they thought about dinner, was deciding on which rooms to inhabit during their stay here. They were really excited to do so and besides, they needed somewhere other than the tiny front hallway to put their luggage. Mignonne grabbed her bags and set off through one of the many newish looking doors going off the living room, hoping to find at least a bathroom to use. The first door, and as a matter of fact, the next three doors, all opened into bedrooms, small in size but really quite charming looking with the gray stone floors and the antique looking furniture. Kitty opened a door on the east side of the living room and found a bathroom with great relief. She'd been wondering out of fear, did they or did they not use bathrooms in Scotland? She didn't remember. Mignonne, at least, found herself hoping that they would eventually find more than one bathroom in this cottage.

After both girls had individually rushed into the bathroom and utilized it, they continued to explore. There were two other doors alongside what Mignonne was now identifying as the *toilette* (thank you, high school French), both opening into other bedrooms. Kitty decided that the tiny room off to the left of the bathroom was speaking to her as her room (?), and she made the decision to claim it.

Mignonne didn't really try to listen *to the voice of the rooms*, so to speak (that mumbo-jumbo was part of Joanna Stone's and it looked like Kitty's weirdness), but she decided that the one other bedroom off this wall next to Kitty's selected room would work for hers. She chose it mostly to keep her in close proximity with her friend; she was desperately grasping at anything familiar right now. Kitty and Mignonne both went in their rooms and looked around, slinging their bags onto the beds and making sure that there were closets or bureaus for their clothes (there were). Before they put anything away, however, Kitty wandered into Mignonne's doorway, breathed in deeply, and looked into Mignonne's eyes as she said, "Well, Miggy, looks like we're here," praying that the excitement would hold out against the anxiety that always accompanied new endeavors for her.

Mignonne, seeming to sense both of her friend's warring emotions, smiled hopefully at Kitty; "Yeah, Kit-Kat, we are. I certainly hope that this doesn't turn out to be a huge mistake of any proportion. This house is great, but I'm still a little wary over what Omage wants us to do for our stay here. I mean, why would this 'order of the Elders' be investing so much money in us, even if we are 'oracles' or whatever? What do you think that even means, anyway?" Not knowing what to say, Kitty just looked wide-eyed and shook her head. "Well, anyway," Mignonne attempted to say nonchalantly as she began to fold and put away her clothes, "we need to eat no matter what happens, so what do you say we see how the kitchen works and make something for dinner?" Kitty's face lit up once Mignonne said this, her finding relief in somebody making even a small semi-solid decision to do something familiar, and her reply was perhaps a little louder and more enthusiastic that she intended. "Sure! Here's hoping there's lots of vegetables! I don't remember if I ever mentioned to Omage that I was a vegetarian, but maybe he assumed such since I'm apparently 'the earth oracle' wooooo." Kitty smiled saucily as she said this, and Mignonne threw the clothes she was putting away into some drawers and followed her through the living room and into the kitchen. Feeling kind of festive, Kitty decided to make a veggie stir-fry for them, since yes, indeed, Omage had had the fridge stocked full of luscious looking fruits and vegetables, accompanied, lo and behold, by a brand new looking wok.

Chapter 11

Discovery

When Kitty and Mignonne woke up in the morning, Kitty at her normal time and Mignonne a little earlier than usual, both went to the kitchen looking around slightly disbelieving at where they were and a little shell-shocked about it. Mignonne decided to make herself a full pot of coffee, not knowing how much would be needed to chill her out. While Kitty fixed herself a bowl of cereal, they chatted unceasingly about trivial things, hoping that this would keep them from panicking since they still had no idea what the day would bring. Finally, Mignonne put the mug that she'd been firmly grasping in both hands down on the table, and Kitty went to the sink to wash and put to dry her cereal bowl. Perhaps he was watching (creepy thought), or maybe he just had a true gift of timing, but at the precise moment that Kitty put her clean bowl and spoon away, Omage knocked on the door. Mignonne knew that it was Omage because she saw him striding vigorously up the walkway through the kitchen window; he knocked on the door, and Mignonne answered at once, still not knowing what this day could possibly bring.

"Madainn mhath," Omage greeted Mignonne before he purposely blew past her and walked into the kitchen; bamboozled over Omage's brisk entrance (*Yes, Omage, please come in*, she thought to herself), and not a little puzzled by the phrase which sounded like something that came out after someone was inebriated, she made a quick mental note to look it up later in the day before she followed after him. Once Mignonne got into the kitchen, Omage seemed to be running some sort of military grade diagnostic of the kitchen, sweeping his eyes of Kitty's clean dishes and Mignonne's still full coffee cup. He seemed almost relieved when he looked around, as though he had expected them to have trashed the place since last night like the slovenly Americans that he felt sure they were. "Mignonne, Kitty," Omage began, "I have come to pick the two of you up to go with me to the Center of the Elders here in Scotland. Here I want to begin showing the two of you your abilities, in preparation for the beginning of training." Here Omage spun around and marched out the kitchen and then out of the house and down the driveway, leaving both Kitty and Mignonne a little miffed (training? In what? And who does he think he is, anyway?! It's barely 9:00 o'clock!). In fact, the girls were a little angry about the whole way that Omage had treated them this morning, but Kitty eventually (after a few other choice words had been exchanged) shrugged and followed Omage outside to his sleek car. Out of habit, Mignonne followed her, her thought percolating to great lengths as to what this day would bring.

On the ride to wherever they were going, Mignonne deduced that they were living about 15 minutes outside of Aberdeen, Scotland (thank you, confusing European street signs), and they seemed to skirt the edges of the city for about half an hour before they reached their destination. With Omage pulling into a vast and remote tract of land, the car turning eventually onto a very nondescript dirt road that eventually arrived at a large stone mansion not unlike the hotel that they'd stayed at, that seemed also newly remodeled, with certain windows having been made shaded and a copious amount of large trees surrounding it for increased privacy. The ride over had been mostly silent, as Omage seemed to have entered into a state of logical, matter-of-fact, let's get this moving determination. When the car finally pulled up in front of the entrance (Mignonne was still not used to this having a driver thing; Kitty, whose family had no car and frequently bummed rides off of people, was not as struck by it), Omage got out and motioned for the girls to follow him up the high entrance stairs and into a long, dark corridor, from which he proceeded to take them into one of the rooms facing behind the entrance. Kitty's head was swimming, and her fear over what was coming grew, but then they arrived at a door that seemed to whine loudly as Omage forced it open.

As they entered through the protesting door, Kitty and Mignonne found themselves in a room with windows facing the side of the house; the room had many odd decorations and an assortment of small, cheesy decorative pieces, but to Kitty's relief it did have a doorway that appeared to lead into an isolated garden area. Mignonne was astounded by the height of the ceiling in the entrance, which was easily sixteen feet or more, and she thought to herself that this ceiling was the only part of this room that made any sense architecturally, epic as the building was and as grand as the grounds appeared to be. Wondering what on earth was about the happen, the girls turned to Omage, who had been joined by two other people, another older man who looked to be of European descent, and a big-boned middle aged woman with thick, almost frizzy dark hair. "Pytel. Aris." Omage motioned from the two individuals to Mignonne and Kitty, "These are two of the oracles; Mignonne, Kitty, these are two members of our order that will be assisting the two of you with coming to grips with your powers." Apparently having accomplished his mission for the day, Omage then turned and just as abruptly as he had arrived at their house that morning, he left the room. It would seem that Omage had a very strong orientation for specific tasks that he needed to accomplish, and once those had been done, he took his ado, Kitty reflected, shaking her head over trying to understand him and his obviously too cool for school mentality. Giving up on finding any kind of solution to the conundrum that was Omage, she turned to face the newcomers, who were being treated to Mignonne's signature glare and seemed more struck by it than Omage had.

"Ladies," Aris began, speaking English well but with a heavy Greek accent, "it is so good to finally have the two of you here. We have no time to waste in preparation for coming confrontations. Mignonne, you will please start out with working with me, and Kitty, please accompany Pytel out into the garden area." *Geez,* thought Mignonne, *are we being prepared for battle or what not? It's like everyone is suddenly treating us like precious commodities in a war or something,* but her ruminations were interrupted by Aris taking her by the arm and pulling her towards one alcove in the room while at the same time briskly motioning for Kitty and Pytel to go outside. Once a super obnoxiously enthusiastic Pytel had almost pushed Kitty out into the garden area, not unlike the way that an overgrown puppy would, Aris turned to Mignonne and quite solemnly closed and opened then opened her eyes. Mignonne was simply relieved to be working a woman (*maybe this wasn't some kind of sadomasochistic sex business,* she thought to herself), even though she normally felt more at ease working with men. Aris sighed and looked away, taking her time as she formed the words.

"I have been a member of the Elders for almost thirty years, and upon entrance each new member must choose which portion of elemental manipulation to study, with only a few standing the influx of time spent in unceasingly perusing a seemingly mundane inquisition, that may never profit us or anyone anything. Ours is a life of study and contemplation, not unlike the practices of a monastery, and many find this to be unswervingly tedious; only a few are privileged enough to begin seeing the intricate beauty in the patterns of all existence. But some, much like the world changing scientists of history, see beauty and long to sculpt the order out of this that we know is present, just not readily apparent to normal human eyes." Aris then met Mignonne's look, as she was trying (really was) to keep paying attention as this woman droned on and on, and she gave Mignonne the most pleasant smile that Mignonne had seen on her face thus far. "I am a student of the ways of *gaoth*, or wind, air, and it is this element's place and purpose in this world that has held an endless fascination for me. I have spent my whole adult life training so that if the oracles did make themselves present during my lifetime, I would be equipped to aid the oracle of gaoth. I find wind, air, and the weather patterns that are produced by it to be overwhelmingly enticing for a program of study. Now, my dear young Oracle, let us begin in our own examination of this topic."

At this point, Aris placed several small and chintzy looking pieces of décor on the side table that was nearby, stepping away while sweeping her hands through the air. "Now Mignonne, let us begin with quite a simple exercise for which it is written that much help comes to the air oracles through. As I'm sure you can see, none of these pieces are valuable or worth keeping in any way, and so I want you to not feel any inhibition about breaking them." Mignonne simply stared at the woman, trying not to show her puzzlement over what she was hearing; what did this person expect her to do? Did this lady really expect her to levitate stuff or something? Mignonne almost laughed thinking this, and she tried only partially successfully to hide her mirth. As it turned out, though, this was precisely what Aris was expecting, and she seemed pleased that Mignonne was catching on. Aris, evidently taking her stifled laughter as happy enthusiasm for what she was saying, smiled again. "Now, I will step back further and let you try to remember a time when you may have found yourself able to do this at certain points in your life; I do not expect you to really move any of these objects, but rather to attempt to recall any point in time where you noticed an increase in wind or air circulation and try and replicate that. Do not worry about time, as we are here as long as you wish or need."

Mignonne couldn't believe what she was hearing; did this lady really expect her to use frickin' *telekinesis?* Or maybe to control the wind like Linka in the television cartoon show *Captain Planet?* As it turned out, her second guess was closer to the truth, although in a way both thoughts applied, and Aris moved backwards, motioning in eager anticipation for Mignonne to begin (begin *what?).* Mignonne had no idea exactly what to do, but she began racking her brains to see if she could remember *any time* when this might have happened; Mignonne desperately searched her memory, and only really came up times when it had been super-hot and muggy outside and she had wished for a breeze, only to have one actualize. When she was a child, she had noted this tendency, but for the life of her she couldn't remember anything funny or strange that she had done at these times; was it certain thoughts? Certain expressive words? Did she jump up and down and clap her hands for crying out loud!? Mignonne didn't know what Aris was waiting for, but she did know that she felt like she was in a stupid situation in a stupid part of the world, and what was she supposed to do anyway? Seeing her puzzlement, Aris soothingly placed her hand on Mignonne's shoulder, "Stop thinking so hard, you'll trip yourself up! You have to stop trying to *think* about what you're doing and let yourself feel the freedom that wind knows." Feeling silly, in desperation Mignonne began eyeballing the objects on the table, willing them to move, please! The items did not in fact move, and in frustration she closed her eyes automatically, feeling pent up animosity towards Omage, Aris, and the whole shooting match. Who cared anyway if she could or couldn't do this? She'd just *go home* and go back to her stupid *normal life!* As she was thinking these things, she mentally placed emphasis on the emphatic phrases, feeling frustration and anger building and fighting against encroaching sorrow, and in defiance all of these pent-up emotions finally released, and she gratefully felt them wash away from her. Suddenly, Mignonne didn't really care what happened right now, and she reached inside herself and found a small, but growing, voice that seemed quite separate from her inside that was speaking to the wind as if it were a person. All at once, she heard the music that is composed in all of the world, and she opened her eyes; the odd items on the table were not moving back and forth per se, but Mignonne was astonished to see that they were vibrating sporadically. Her astonishment at this broke the wave of emotion that was going through her head and heart, and the vibration subsequently ceased. *What had just happened? What had she done? Are you telling me that Omage might be onto the truth?* She thought all of these things rapidly, glancing furtively up at Aris, who was smiling triumphantly. "Good, Mignonne!" Aris clapped her hands together, "that is certainly a start! I see that Omage was right after all! Do not worry, we will work on this. By the end of our sessions together, you should be able to command the air, which is the most abundant and everlastingly essential of all the elements. It moves freely whither it wills, and by the end of our times together it will move wherever you should wish." Feeling as if she was being patronized about what had happened, Mignonne felt her frustration and a passionate desire to succeed at everything overflow, and when she stopped trying to cause movement, she felt energy leave her body and explode across the small table, sending all of the knickknacks flying onto the floor and shattering.

At the same time that Aris was beginning what Mignonne thought of as her trial by fire (there was no fire, true, but this was impossible!), Kitty accompanied Pytel outside, her nerves about the whole situation not being much helped by the beauty surrounding her. The garden area was designed to inspire freedom, in spite of the tall limestone walls that surrounded it. Cedar trees, birch trees, and super tall Douglas firs each filled various spots along the border of the garden, and their very height made Kitty feel their freedom, in spite of them being boxed in technically in the garden. Thistles and witch hazels carpeted the ground, and only a tiny space had been cleared between them to create a walking path that led to a small square of land which had been cleared out so give access to what looked like a simple patch of untilled earth. Kitty followed Pytel's example and knelt next to this small swath of earth, instinctively reaching her hands into the soil and marveling at its richness. "I see you are making yourself quite at home, O Oracle of Delphi," Pytel smiled teasingly at his own words. And when Kitty started and immediately pulled out of the earth with her hands, only managing to sputter out, "What did you just call me?" quite indignant over being called outside her name once again with strange gibberish. Pytel looked apologetic as he said, "Simply an ancient Greek name for the head representative of the temple of the earth spirit Python; not an absolutely exact moniker, but you catch my drift," was Pytel's lilting response as he waved away the statement, as if neither it nor the ancient story was of any importance. He smiled again as he began a speech that he had quite obviously been rehearsing to give for years.

"Anyway, I thought that this garden would please you and make it easier for you to tap into your abilities as earth oracle. I see you already have an attraction to the verifiable life that it in the very essence of the land, and that will do well for helping us. Omage has told me that you already have a garden of your own at your home, and I am sure that you tend this garden with unending care and love; while this undoubtedly brings about much success with growth and prospering plants when tended in the normal way, we are together going to try and accelerate that process." Pytel gently tipped a packet of wildflower seeds into Kitty's hand, sitting back and speaking softly and in a soothing manner to Kitty; "I have given you some common seeds to begin with, and though the inner intrinsic complexity of these and all seeds will no doubt baffle you at first, I want you to simply to hold these seeds in your hand, close your eyes, and sit back and listen to the voices that are calling out from each tiny container of life, from the portions of existence that the eye does not naturally look at, at the very center of what makes these seeds alive, so that you will be able to access the strength that God has given to each of these, and use your natural strengths to encourage a more rapid development. Wildflowers have no order and need no set diameters, so I thought these would be simpler for you to start with. Take these seeds, *listen* to them, and then try to plant and manipulate growth in them."

Very much confused, Kitty couldn't help but remember her mother's admonishments that plants and over greenery were highly attune to the aura of the people who were planting them, and this had a direct impact on their posterity. She had always laughed and written this off as another one of her mother's bonkers ideas, but it caught her attention that people like the ones who belonged to this *order* might agree. Of course, she had found that vegetables and flowers did tend to do better when you stopped trying to move along conventional lines and tried to meet the individual needs of the particular plant that you were working with, almost sensing what that individual plant needed and going about to meet those needs, but she had always chalked that up to simple common sense. *But maybe it wasn't so common?* Kitty gently started shifting the seeds from one hand to the other, and her mind went blank as she felt the coarseness or the smoothness of these various seeds, her ears picking up on the tiny rustling sounds that accompanied their imperceptible movement, finding peace in the order in which they moved now and had been moving for eons.

Most people would not have found order in what looked like the entirely sporadic shifting among the handful of seeds in Kitty's hand, but when she naturally shut herself off from the world around her, as she did at her garden at home, and paid sole attention to the seeds, she could almost hear them humming and crying for earth to give them life. Without thinking, Kitty dug out several little crevices in the soil, and gently slid the seeds in her hand into these places. After she had gently covered the seeds with earth, Kitty sat back and in-stinctively cocked her head to the side as she had always done when gardening, but this time she tried and listened for the tiny voices of life that Pytel said were present. At first she wondered, were they really? It seemed as if she could hear them, but was she imagining it? Her overactive imagination giving to her what she had been told to expect? Kitty didn't know, but she tried to clear her mind as she placed her hands over the soil spots, not thinking but listening with joy to the song of the earth as it became increasingly clear to her. It was only when she cleared her mind entirely and simply embraced the harmony that she heard in the seeds that she found herself wanting this growth to be made manifest, to *happen*; this nudging impatience grew and welled up inside of her, until she was quite positive that she would overflow with whatever this new energy inside of her was. She wanted to contain this energy, because she somehow felt that it was not supposed to come out, but it grew, and grew, and got to the point where she was no longer able to restrain it, and as it tipped over the edges of her consciousness, Kitty gave in to its escape. She simply sat back and let it overflow off her, trickling down from her center at her heart, coming off her head, and washing over the earth in front of her. When Kitty moved her hands off of the earth, she somehow was not at all astounded to find that tiny green tendrils were now pushing through the earth where the seeds had been placed, and she rejoiced alongside these seeds at their approaching life.

Kitty and Mignonne continued working with their instructors for only a few more hours that day, feeling so exhausted at the end that they were unable to see straight (this figure of speech might not be *technically* true, but considering the trouble both girls had with walking at the end it might be an appropriate description). Though the girls both longed to go to a soft bed and collapse at the end of this, Omage apparently wanted to speak to them and they were left together in what they assumed was his office. Tired though they were, upon seeing each other both girls began babbling on and on about what had happened that day, what they had seen and what they had somehow *done*. The girls were interrupted by Omage, who stopped at the door and began slowly bringing his hands together, in what was supposed to be a slow form of clapping that could have been seen as mocking. Kitty and Mignonne looked at him, Kitty with anticipation stemming from the positive things that had happened that day and Mignonne with pent up anger (*how dare he put them through this! The fact that this day had brought many exciting revelations didn't matter! And what was he doing? The sarcastic slow-clap!?*). Anyway, what happened eventually was that Omage smiled like a truly socially awkward adolescent after this and then walked into the office space (Kitty thought this for lack of a better descriptive word).

"Ladies! I am so pleased to see you two at the end of your first day of skill development! From what Aris and Pytel have told me pertaining to both of your abilities to create cause and the subsequent effects within respective components of your elements, I am truly pleased! You both show so much promise with being able to master your respective abilities, in fact, so much so that I am of the opinion that you both are ready for what I have to tell the Oracles." Here Omage looked suddenly solemn and clasped his hand in front of him. He seemed to be waging a fierce inner battle with himself, debating whether to tell them right now or wait for a time when they were not so exhausted. Mignonne saw this and dearly wished that the quite obvious stick figures who were grappling inside his head would have a winner, so he would figure something out already so they could go back to their place (she still couldn't see it as "home" yet). Of course, after only a few moments one side of Omage did win, and he apparently ended up deciding to wait on telling them whatever it was. Omage smiled, a little falsely this time, and in an overly enthusiastic voice said, "Well, there's plenty of time for that in the coming days. It might be better if I waited until all of you were gathered together, so I will be able to tell everyone myself, and not risk someone receiving misinformation because of hearsay. I simply wanted to tell the two of you definitely about the fact that the two of you shall have a roommate soon! I hope that the fact that it will be a male shouldn't be a problem?" Apparently, the fact that this might bother one or both of them had only just dawned on Omage, and he looked at them apprehensively. Mignonne shrugged like it was non-issue (she had a dad and a little brother, after all, and was used to cohabiting with the male of the species). Kitty however breathed in a little sharply and looked at Omage with worried eyes (*she* had only experienced life in close proximity with males by staying at the same house with Mignonne's family, and even that hadn't happened very frequently. She saw Mignonne's father and brother largely as posters standing in the corner of a life that she could escape easily, should she so choose). Taking the lack of response as a good response, Omage started prattling on about the new oracle who the Elders had discovered and who had agreed to move from the U.S. to Scotland. "I think he will be a good adjustment to the two of you living in close proximity with the other oracles. First, he is from the United States, so you will not have to adapt already to a person of a new culture or background living in your house. Second, he is quite a nice, mild young man who I do not believe will present any problems for the two of you." Kitty and Mignonne exchanged resigned glances with each other; so much had so recently changed in their life, they couldn't imagine a new roommate being a huge issue. I mean, next to moving to a new country and discovering inner traits about themselves that they still couldn't believe having a new person in their lives seemed to be a nonissue (unless, of course, that new roommate turned out to be an insane pyrotechnician or something). Escaping the room before the girls could ask any questions, Omage paused at the door, seeming to remember something that would be of importance for them to hear. "He is expected to arrive within the week, making final decisions about his life back in the States, you know. I will keep you two posted." At this, Omage vanished into the hallway, and Kitty and Mignonne suddenly remembered their exhaustion, groaned in response to their overly stressed heads, and went out the front door to the car which was there to take them "home."

Chapter 12

Water

The girls were driven home by one of the same Elders who had accompanied Omage to pick them up at the airport (Kitty wasn't certain which one it was though; Philippe? Adair?), and they promptly set about trying to relax. Kitty went directly to the kitchen and began chopping up *more* assorted vegetables, comforted by the fact that these veggies remained entirely in their dead (though fresh) state under her ministrations. Mignonne wasn't able to escape the air, but went upstairs and drew a hot bath, sinking into it and forcing her mind to stop running on and on over what had happened that day. Emerging from the bath (the water got cold so fast) and wrapping a towel around herself, Mignonne shuffled to her room and threw on some adult sized cartoon jammies (Mrs. Johansen had bought these for her last birthday, as a joke? Maybe?), that even with their absurd character drawings, were super cozy, and she walked into the kitchen where Kitty was chopping squash as if her life depended on it. "Here, Kit-Kat, let me help, before you're purely responsible for the massacre and mutilation of root vegetables," Mignonne smiled and grabbed a knife out of one of the drawers, and to her relief this statement/action *did* have the desired effect of making Kitty laugh. "Thanks, Miggy, but I've only got one more chop, and then I'll put everything in a pot, if I can find a big enough one, and then I'll boil them with salt and pepper, maybe pop some corn, and get the tea going at the same time." Kitty smiled weakly at this statement but still seemed to be fighting back tears, so Mignonne did what she normally did in these situations; sometimes she knew that you just have to take control of these situations with Kitty before she went off the deep end. Mignonne took the knife from Kitty, frog marching her out of the room, instructing her to go take a calming shower, or to do what usually worked better for Kitty and go sit outside and *chill*. Kitty seemed to think that the latter would have a better effect, and so she quite willingly left the dinner in Mignonne's hands and went out (not to the garden, she'd had enough of that today, bleh), but to a close neighboring field, just walking around and looking at the lands that were connected to their house. After about ten minutes, she had calmed down and was walking back towards the house when she saw, feeling distress about this at first, the same car that she and Mignonne had been picked up with at the airport in coming down their small driveway.

Rapidly exiting the car, Omage immediately rushed to the front door, walking so hurriedly that Kitty had not even managed to catch up and she made her way back to the entrance way a little behind him. He banged quite emphatically on the door, and when Kitty came running up behind him and clapped him on the shoulder, Omage startled a bit. "Gah!" Omage said in surprise, but upon seeing Kitty immediately relaxed; Kitty opened the door and motioned for Omage to come in, staring at him and looking quite puzzled Why had he come today? Didn't today have enough of a shock to it, sheesh. Omage made quick steps as he briskly proceeded down the hallway, turning into the living area without pause, as though quite expecting for Kitty and Mignonne, who had just emerged from the kitchen, to follow. Mignonne and Kitty both felt like Omage would really need to work on his assumptions about people behaving strictly as he expected;

surprise might do him good sometimes. With this in mind, neither Kitty nor Mignonne entered the living area, but rather remained standing in the doorway, arms crossed and eyes narrowed. Omage saw what they were doing and sighed slightly, evidently not expecting much besides mild belligerence from them after their first day of training. Mignonne noticed that his eyes looked a little strained, like he'd been focusing very hard on something and could really use a little peace and quiet. *Geez*, she thought, *we're stressed and tired too, dude, why not wait until **tomorrow** to tell us whatever the reason that you're here is?* In her mind, nothing was important enough to warrant his *continued* presence in their life today. Kitty too was eyeing Omage warily, finally skirting into room and cautiously perching on the desk in the corner, watching him as one might watch a wild animal they encountered, moving cautiously so to make an escape should it choose to attack. Omage raised his hands to his face and began rubbing his eyes, and apparently finally decided that it would be better for everyone concerned to go ahead and get this over with.

"Ladies," Omage finally managed to breathe out, "I know that this has been an enormous day for the two of you, and believe me, I deeply regret impeding on your time of relaxation tonight." He looked like he too, could've used a break tonight, but he continued doggedly on. "However, circumstances have altered a bit, and it is necessary for me to come over and see the two of you once again today." These words were muffled by Omage's hands, which he kept up at his head, massaging his eyes and his temples; it appeared that his exuberance from earlier in the day was gone, leaving him with an accepting, if resigned and weary, attitude about something. "It became necessary that I come to see the two of you again today because the Elders have had a new development in our continuing search to find and unite the oracles. We have located the oracle of water and are currently in the process of bringing him here. Evidently, he took matters into his own hands and went ahead and purchased a plane ticket to come here, and he is arriving much ahead of our schedule that we had set for him. We have spoken to this young man, and had been attempting to bring him here, but he has proved to be much more resistant to this move than the two of you were. I have spoken to him, but I do not know to what extent he believes me, even after I gave him a similar tonic to the one that I gave the two of you and he saw the manifestations of his gift. He seems to be entertaining the idea that this whole thing is a joke, with us going to the trouble of manipulating seltzers to produce the effect that we desire. But be that as it is, he has agreed to come over; granted, he is trying to remain in control of the situation and come over on *his* time. It has not been the trek that the two of you undertook from the United States, him being located much closer in England, and he seems to be entertaining the idea that this is an elaborate hoax that someone dreamed up and is implementing in his life. He seems to be toying with the idea that he'd rather just get this over with, whatever the 'prank' may be."

"Hold up, hold up, hold up," Mignonne growled in frustration, "Okay, I get it, *the order of the Elders* (here she used sarcastic finger quotation marks) has found somebody else to bring here in order to discover our *true purpose*, but did you guys just start looking for everyone or something? It seems kind of random that you are finding everyone *right this instant!* And even if you have found a new person to bring here, why come tonight and tell us!? It just seems like this could have waited until a more opportune time, like tomorrow!" Here Mignonne decided to give up her little rant, panting as if she'd just run a race and desperately trying to remember if she had forgotten to tell Omage anything of importance. Seriously, why couldn't this dude leave them alone and let them rest!? If this was going to be his constant behavior while they were in Scotland, Mignonne really couldn't see herself staying and dealing with it for long. Even more frustrating, Omage seemed suddenly quite amused by her outburst, and tried to make sympathetic eye contact with Kitty, shaking his head as though he pitied her for having such a high strung friend. Kitty didn't like whatever assumptions he was making, and she certainly didn't want him to think that she was the rational, quiet friend who he could connect with. Kitty locked eyes with Omage and tried to communicate the full force of her hostility to him: *losing patience, Omage. Either get to a point or get out* her expression seemed to be trying send over to him. Seeming to get this message, Omage raised his hands in front of his face and laughed a little, shaking his head over everything that was happening. "I come to see you so much later after what was, I'm certain, an exhausting day to tell you this because I do not know exactly when this water oracle will arrive here, not having purchased the plane tickets myself. And I simply didn't want the two of you to be taken unawares, should he and a member of the Elders show up at an inopportune time, such as the middle of the night tonight. Should anyone enter this house at a time when the two of you are unaware, please do not panic. We are simply bringing the water oracle over at whatever time he gets here. This could be tonight, could be tomorrow, who knows?" Omage made his way to the door after making this pronouncement, turning to Kitty and Mignonne, who had followed him down the hall, at the door, and behaving most strangely. He turned and grasped Mignonne's hand, bringing it to his lips and quickly brushing a light kiss against it. "Mignonne, Kitty, as always it has been a pleasure to see the two of you, and I will leave you now. I just couldn't forgive myself if the two of you weren't warned about approaching events." He smiled sheepishly as he said this, seeming to wish to escape their stares because he turned right after and dashed out the door into his waiting car. Mignonne looked at Kitty wide-eyed. "What is his deal?" she finally said, "I hope he doesn't think that he can come here whenever and we'll automatically be okay with it! I mean come on, he couldn't have told us this before we left today?" Mignonne was quite angry at herself that heart had started racing a little as he took and kissed her hand, but she supposed this was only because this wasn't a common gesture in the States. Looking thoughtful, Kitty finally mused "Well, I don't know. Maybe he didn't know until now, you never know." Kitty didn't want to become

Omage's friendly face of the oracles, but she couldn't ignore the logic of what she was thinking. "Whatever," stuttered Mignonne, shaking her head in exasperation, "I'm going to make some sugary black tea and then go to bed. Today's been weird enough, and I absolutely refuse to deal with anything or anyone else." Mignonne turned at this and stalked into the kitchen, pouring a cup of tea out of the kettle on the stove into a mug with some granulated sugar inside it, after which she turned and went rushing into her room. Kitty felt like she also had much to ponder, so she also went and filled a cup of tea (with honey, not sugar), and went into her room, deciding that *now* was a really good time for that warm relaxing bath.

Even though the two worried a little (Kitty especially) that Omage or some member of the Elders would come barging into the house sometime in the middle of the night, this did not happen, for which they were very thankful. The next morning Mignonne still stepped out of her room looking warily around; she really didn't want some random guy to catch her wearing just a baggy t-shirt with morning breath. Seeing the coast clear, she went to the bathroom that she and Kitty had been using (closest to their rooms, thank goodness), her thankfulness that no one else appeared to be in the house lasted until she got to the bathroom door. She had just placed her hand on the doorknob when the bathroom door jerked abruptly open, almost pulling her down to the floor. She shrieked in surprise, while Kitty (the perpetrator) also yelled in surprise, and Mignonne quickly stood up and looked at Kitty as Kitty was attempting to leave the bathroom. Neither girl had altogether gotten over the unexpected upheaval, and as Mignonne tried to calm her breathing she looked at Kitty. Kitty's breath came rapidly, but suddenly her mouth twitched like she was fighting a smile. Mignonne wasn't able to contain the mirth that she felt welling up inside her at this, and without any spoken words Kitty and Mignonne both started laughing hysterically, bending over and fighting for breath, fighting to stay upright throughout this moment of revelry. "Oh, Mignonne!" Kitty finally gasped out, "I so needed that! Just letting go, for even just a second, helps!" "Yeah, it so does," was Mignonne's rejoinder. "If we can laugh like that over something so stupid and unimportant, maybe everything will be okay, even if Omage does bring a raving psychopath or something to live here with us." Both girls still breathing hard and smiling, at this Kitty walked to her room to get dressed with a much lighter heart than before, and Mignonne found that her morning routine wasn't as laced with dread as it might have been otherwise.

Even after this morning hilarity, much of that day was not a laughing matter. After Adair picked them up that morning and took them to the place of the Elders' insanity (Mignonne couldn't get this name that she came up with out of her head; it seemed appropriate), the morning and rest of the day were quite strenuous. Apparently, having decided amongst themselves that Kitty and Mignonne were indeed members of the Oracles, Aris and Pytel proceeded this day to put the two of them through an even more exhausting battery of training methods. Mignonne wasn't just asked if she could try to make the objects on the table wiggle, but if she could make them *levitate;* this put a lot of strain on her mind in every possible way, and her brain felt like it was going through a really intense strength training exercise, like she was at a gym for her brain. Kitty was not faring much better, with Pytel seeming to drop his attitude of exuberant happiness and really focus in on directing her to actually make things grow to a certain height and then to force the tendrils and branches to move into various positions and shapes. Kitty and Mignonne found themselves exhausted over the next several days, as they were being forced to make their minds form alterations and speed up processes that are really not possible. So tired were they from everything that they forgot to worry about their new "roommate" coming and simply tried to make them themselves keep working through a lot of fatigue. Five days, then a week, had passed in the blink of an eye, and Kitty and Mignonne found themselves wondering in down time (rare) about how this lifestyle had quickly become so real to them. When this thought occurred to them both girls tried to remember to shoot at least a text message or a short call to their family members back in the States, but as training kept intensifying this was able to happen much less often. Mignonne and Kitty were thankful when they were each given a day off of training to recuperate, and it was on this day that Omage again appeared at their house one afternoon, accompanied by a young gentleman with tousled dark hair whose eyes looked like they were kind, but still watched everything and everyone with wariness.

Kitty and Mignonne had been so overjoyed about their day off that they were not thinking about the arrival of their new housemate. Surprisingly enough, Kitty was inside making some of her patented fruit smoothies in a blender that she had found hidden among the kitchen tools, while Mignonne was laid out in the light of a living room window and enjoying the late afternoon sun, wearing a pair of large red sunglasses and a white wicker hat. They were pondering anything except Omage and the order when his car pulled up and he and a person they'd never seen before exited the vehicle. Mignonne jumped to her feet upon hearing their approach and stood in the front doorway staring at them as they walked up. "Mignonne!" called out Omage, sounding like he was working hard at making himself sound cheery, his voice making a lot of unnecessary undulations in speech, "I am so glad to see you! I wanted to introduce you and Kitty to the first of your fellow oracles that we have located and are bringing here! I hope that the three of you will work together in order to form a band of friends who are able to combat any darkness!" *What is he talking about?* Mignonne found herself pondering on once again; she had noticed that this was a normal thought when she was attempting to interpret Omage's speech. Noticing that Omage's words seemed to be not really genuine, but rather forcefully cheery, Omage was talking about everything in a way that led her to believe that he probably had a good deal riding on whether this "mission" worked or out, though she could not possibly imagine what it could be. Acting really desperate to get away from the house and them, Omage turned to

Taylor and the luggage that had just been unloaded from the car. Omage spoke softly to him before he turned and gave Kitty and Mignonne a farewell wave, then climbed back into the automobile. The driver quickly put the car in reverse and then floored it back down the drive. Kitty, Mignonne, and Taylor stood there staring at each other for a brief moment, and then Kitty took the first step of forming a possible camaraderie.

"Taylor, is it?" Kitty spoke brightly and openly, "How 'bout Miggy and I help you to move your suitcases inside and then you can join us for a homemade smoothie? Or maybe you'd like to get settled in first?" Kitty exclaimed rapidly but not unkindly, trying to speak in a very nonthreatening manner. Mignonne threw a grateful glance Kitty's way and then also looked at this newcomer, who seemed really stunned and unable to speak at this moment. Mignonne stepped forward and grabbed one of his bags, also trying to put him more at his ease by saying nonchalantly "Yeah, follow me. You can pick out which of the three bedrooms on this other side of the house that you'd like." Actually eternally thankful that he had not lunged at her as she reached down to grab his suitcase, Mignonne picked up the bag, turned, and motioned for Taylor to follow her inside away from the entranceway. Taylor looked very dumbstruck, but Kitty attributed that to the simple fact of the whole strangeness of the situation and did not question it, deciding that this was one of those situations where you had to move slowly and cautiously with the someone and not overwhelm them with too much too soon. She imagined while making these first interactions that Taylor was indeed a member of some distant Aboriginal tribe who was entirely unfamiliar with her ways, and this helped enormously while she and Mignonne were making the first points of contact with this bizarre, quiet, but seemingly nonaggressive being.

Taylor muttered something that sounded kind of like "okay," and held most of his luggage while they walked inside. Mignonne was horribly bad at small talk, so she didn't even attempt it, deciding to stay silent while they progressed into the hallway and towards the other three bedrooms that were located off the living room. Taylor peered into each room, and he surprised them by dissolving into laughter when he looked into the third room. He hooted and threw his head back while laughing really loudly, and since laughter and smiles are contagious, Mignonne and Kitty also relaxed and smiled, looking at each other and shrugging because of a failure to understand what was happening. *Did he have tourette's?* Kitty anxiously wondered even as she was smiling, because if he did, she and Mignonne had no idea how to work with someone like that. While Kitty was hurriedly racking her brain over some of Joanna Stone's ravings and written journal articles about the care and consideration that was due to the mentally different, Taylor finally rose from a crouching position and turned to the girls, wiping the tears out of his eyes as he addressed them for the first time. "I'm sorry, girls," he trilled out musically, reminding Mignonne of the flowing of a very calm, but still active, body of running water moving sedately over rocks and tree branches. She figured that this was probably because she thought that Omage had mentioned that this was this water oracle, and her brain was desperately trying to understand this new person and fill in the appropriate gaps with what she figured was right? Anyway, Taylor got control of himself as he moved into one of the bedrooms, throwing a suitcase down on the bed. "It's just that this room, I mean the paint color, the furniture style, everything, reminds me a lot of a bedroom that I had as a child, and it really threw me for a loop to see that here. Maybe these Elders have been too much in our heads after all." Taylor turned and gave the two ladies a very genuine smile as he seemed to make the decision that these circumstances were not threatening and that he was okay to be himself. Mignonne and Kitty looked at Taylor very surprised and a little bit like they had been thrown off guard and weren't quite understanding the situation, but they tentatively returned his smile and put his possessions down.

Taylor might not be the most exuberant guy in the world, but in a couple of hours he seemed to really warm up to this new situation of existing alongside the two girls, who he saw were also trying to get a handle on what was happening. He unpacked his suitcases in his room that afternoon, and Kitty and Mignonne tried to relax; they found that they were even going so far as to muffle their voices to whispers and move around the house cautiously, but this wasn't because of anything that Taylor was doing. Mignonne figured it had to be a natural response to living with someone new who you hadn't met before; probably had to be a lot like moving into a new dorm room at college, although Mignonne admitted to herself that she didn't actually have that experience, she was just supposing. Kitty and Mignonne tried to stop obsessing for a little while and lost themselves in a vapid sitcom (apparently Scotland had those too). And about an hour after Taylor had gone into his room, he edged into the living room and sat down. Mignonne asked him if he'd prefer anything else on TV, to be nice, but Taylor shook his head no and sat there quietly for a few seconds, but then decided that it was better to face the worst possible scenario than stay sitting on the couch without saying anything. Kitty and Mignonne would later learn that this *better to do or die* attitude was quite common for Taylor, who seemed to exist in a constant state of fluctuation, making big decisions quickly not being his strong point. Taylor sat up a little straighter, took a drink of the water that he'd brought from the kitchen, and looked at Mignonne and Kitty, trying to maintain eye contact throughout his disclosure. Kitty went ahead and turned off the TV, seeing that he was wanting to say something.

"Kitty, Mignonne," Taylor began, a trifle tremulously, with a lilting British accent. "I'd like the three of us to be friends, since apparently we're going to be living together for at least a little while and training with the Elders. I think that would make life simpler. So just to go ahead and clear up some immediate questions, my name is Taylor Murphy. I'm 19 years old, and until now I've lived with my grandparents. Long story for another time," Taylor stated matter-of-factly with an upraised hand when he saw that Mignonne was about to ask about this. "I was actually raised until I was eight in upstate New York, but my grandparents put me through some kind of weird private school after that that taught all kinds of bizarre esoteric stuff, and so I vaguely knew about orders and traditions that believed in our sort of oddity, but I never once thought that *I* would get so mixed up in that." Taylor sat back and smiled ruefully at this before he began again. "It's true that I've always loved being near the water, but in the part of England where my grandparents live you don't see a lot of it, apart from the private pools and stuff. Anyway, long story short, I decided to take a year off from school after high school and 'find myself' (Taylor made air quotation marks here). But recently I got a letter from someone at the University of Glasgow, asking me to come visit the campus, meeting first with a representative from the school. I figured, 'What the hell?' so I packed up and came and the Elders all told me this super weird story about the oracles. I decided eventually after returning home that I had nothing to lose by coming, so I came, but on my time, not theirs." Taylor smiled sardonically as he said this last statement, shrugging resignedly like coming here was better than staying home. Mignonne and Kitty were both bursting with questions, but something about the way that Taylor made his last statement let them know that he was done talking about his past and would not welcome those inquiries. They resigned themselves to just being curious for a while; Mignonne figured he'd tell them eventually if he wanted, even though patience was not her strongest character trait and so she struggled with this. Kitty tried to dwell on Joanna Stone's 'Respect Other's Privacy' mantra, despite her curiosity; her mom always was really focused on the fact of respecting barriers that others put up, and not to be a nosy-nelly. Kitty was truly trying to adhere to this, since it seemed to work better with a lot of people than rough demanding. It turned out to be a good thing that neither girl pressed Taylor on this, as he generally used a person's ability to stay quiet and listen to gage how well he'd get along with them, and he was learning, not only from the Elders, but from his own sneaking suspicion, that he, Kitty, and Mignonne really, *really* needed eventually to get along well. Apparently, this was it for Taylor's disclosure for this time, with him feeling like he'd shared all necessary information and the two girls could do with this information as they would.

Chapter 13

Life with Three

Kitty found that the addition of another being (a dude, no less) to be an extreme departure from home life as she knew it. Coming from a single parent household, she had found living with Mignonne to be not that different from her experiences with the homey cottage of her childhood since they spent so much time avoiding the twins, and Mignonne's parents weren't really hovering. Adding Taylor was a whole different world though, and while he did really try not to add chaos or disorder, it seemed that these things were perpetually stalking him. Indeed, every little day to day life detail seemed to be haunted for him by the incumbent possibility of flying off the handle with him and not behaving in a normal way. For instance, one morning, Kitty and Mignonne were heading downstairs to eat some breakfast before their day of "training" to which Taylor had started accompanying them, began, when Taylor inadvertently chose right that moment that the girls were in the hall in fling the bathroom door open, revealing him wrapped up in a towel with another towel covering his hair. This wouldn't have been anything to worry about, had he not slammed the door open on the approaching Kitty's face, causing Mignonne to shriek and jump back, surprising Taylor to the point to where he slipped on the edge of the floor leading into the hallway, where it transitioned from tile to wood. He lost hold of his toiletries basket (dark wicker, actually pretty nice looking for a man's bathroom bag), and his legs flew out from under him. And Taylor actually landed on the wet bathroom tile, looking that he had no clue what had happened or why he was where he was. Mignonne immediately put her arms around Kitty, who was leaning over favoring a very bruised nose, and looked with scorn and anger at the prostrate Taylor on the ground. No one said anything for about half a minute, with Taylor looking with fear at Kitty and Mignonne, surely thinking that he had just ruined any possibility of friendship with his new roommates; while he was staring petrified at Kitty who was leaning over with Mignonne's arm across her shoulder, the best possible thing happened. Kitty began softly (her nose wouldn't allow for anything more exuberant) to chuckle slowly, as if she couldn't believe the predicament that had happened and remembering how there a been a similar situation with her and Mignonne upon their first arriving. Her chuckles grew more pronounced. And when it dawned on Mignonne what was happening she also began to giggle, her attempt at containing her mirth eventually breaking through into a full, rocking laugh. Taylor was staring bewildered at the girls, neither of whom appeared to be in control of themselves. "You look completely ridiculous, Taylor! What's on your head, some kind of old school afternoon bonnet?" At this Mignonne completely lost control again, propping up on a wall to keep herself from toppling down the stairs as she convulsed with laughter. Taylor (who they were learning was very perceptive) saw and accepted this atmospheric change, and before he even pulled himself off the floor made his most diva-esque head toss. "Why yes, Mignonne. I always wear a bonnet when exiting the bathroom; it's quite stylish, see?" At this statement, Taylor rose from the floor and made an exaggerated partial pirouette, keeping one hand on the towel around his waist so to avoid any more embarrassing fiascos, finishing off by saying, "Good day to you both," and scurrying down the hall and into his bedroom. Even though Kitty's eyes were still slightly watering and the marks on her nose promised to bruise, she shook her head and smiled as she and Mignonne made their way downstairs. She hoped that her days of bathroom fiascos might be done, though she was quite grateful for this one.

As Mignonne was putting the beans in the coffee grinder to make her morning hit of caffeine, after she and Kitty had successfully made it to the kitchen without any more Taylor-turmoil, she hesitantly turned and faced her friend, who was still massaging her nose. "Kitty?" she began as if she didn't quite know anything else to say, "Are you making any progress on your oracle abilities? I'm not sure that I am, and what if Omage recognizes this and sends me home? Would you be okay here with Taylor? And what am I supposed to do if I get sent back home?! It's a little late to apply for college this year, so I guess I could get a part-time job…" Mignonne said this with obvious distaste; even though she was very friendly and hardworking, she seemed always to clash in whatever job she got, even babysitting the neighbors' kids on Saturdays. She was fine as long as they had a strict daily itinerary to stick to, but she'd rather face an impromptu Algebra exam than face a totally blank day with the kids (her siblings included). Kitty looked nervously at Mignonne, and her voice trembled as she managed to squeak out, "I don't really know if I am either; that first day it all seemed like it was going to be so natural and easy, but I don't know now. And no, I don't want to be left in foreign country with strangers, thank you very much. If you get sent back, I'll have to go, too. I don't know what this would be like if I was completely alone doing it." Something about saying this seemed to brighten up Kitty's spirits though, and she smiled pretty broadly and said with obvious relief on the thinking, "I'm sure that won't happen though; Omage said that this wasn't going to be simple. He can't expect us to know more than we do; we've only been here for a few weeks." Mignonne nodded her head at this, as if hoping against hope that it was so. A new figure appeared at the entrance of the kitchen; Taylor, freshly showered with damp hair and actually clothed in jeans and a button-down shirt that he hadn't bothered to tuck in, placed his hands sort of defiantly in his pockets and made eye contact with Mignonne. And almost forcefully, as if he was willing himself to believe this, with short and clipped statements said, "Everything is fine, Mignonne. I haven't been here as long as the two of you, and I don't even think that I've had a really good practice day like the two of you apparently had. I'm not sure that anything is happening when I try to 'manipulate water,' but it's all going to turn out okay. The Elders obviously had some sort of idea of how to find us, and now I hope that they have a pretty good grasp on how to train us, so it's on them if this doesn't work out. *They* are the ones who've wasted a lot of time and money if we're not meeting their, here again with the air quotes, '*expectations*.' It's totally not on us if this doesn't work out, but I'm betting that it will." Taylor smiled hopefully and moved to the fridge to grab some orange juice, saying in a muffled voice while his head was inside the fridge, "Besides, from what I've overheard them saying when they didn't think I was listening, you two are doing fine. They're especially pleased with the rate at which you're progressing, Kitty." Taylor smiled and swigged his juice while he met Kitty's gaze; he did have a fun goofy smile, she thought. Though Mignonne was a trifle miffed, not that he'd said good things about Kitty but because he *hadn't* said anything, let alone anything good, about her, she put the fresh coffee in a to-go thermos and she, Kitty, and Taylor all walked out on the porch to await the arrival of their daily ride to shuttle them to the domain of the Elders.

Once the car had picked them up that morning, dropping them off at the Elders' domicile, it was with something a little like dread that Mignonne got out of the car. *What if she still couldn't do it today? What if she couldn't do it ever?* Mignonne found herself pondering as she came off of the smile high that Taylor's words had induced; she was wearing mascara, eye liner, and lip gloss, a sure sign that she was feeling uncomfortable; when she was chill, she didn't bother with makeup, but she did tend to wear it as a defense mechanism when she wasn't. The makeup face mask wasn't making her feel any better about her abilities, but it did have the advantage of concealing any abject worry that she might be feeling (at least she hoped it did). As they were walking up the stairs to go in, Kitty was having trouble walking straight, her distracted mind apparently not communicating any longer with her body about a trifling thing like *walking*. When the girls glanced at Taylor, he seemed very calm, his expression set and determined, whatever he might have been feeling on the inside. He looked like he about to face off with someone in the gladiatorial ring, and he looked resigned but determined not to lose face. Mignonne envied him this confidence, whether it was real or not, and she also envied Kitty's distracted, seemingly serene clumsiness. She suddenly stopped herself from thinking these envious thoughts, chiding herself that they were immature and uncalled for, and she wasn't a twelve year old brat for goodness' sake. Trying to shake this thought, when the three of them reached the doorway Mignonne, Kitty, and Taylor all paused for a second to look at one another, gathering courage and strength from the others. If one of them didn't know anything about what was happening, at least they weren't alone, after all. Opening the door and walking in, Kitty found herself wondering absentmindedly if this sudden feeling of stamina and camaraderie was just in her head? Or did the others feel better too? *Oh well*, she finally decided; *it didn't really matter*. What mattered was the day ahead, and Mignonne had almost made up her mind to confront Omage about everything when they found themselves walking into a hallway with all of the windows covered and the lights dimmed, as if to communicate immediately that this day called for a solemn attitude without any childish antics. Taylor gave they two a wondering look, as if he was trying to ask mentally if they knew anything about what was happening. Mignonne shrugged her shoulders, and Kitty didn't even notice Taylor's glance. Apparently, she was trying to see if she could make out anything through the darkness in the facility that got more pronounced as the hallway progressed, and she was instinctively trying to always check her vicinity for immediate threats.

Chapter 14

The Tribunal

While the three Oracles made their way tentatively down the hallway, Mignonne registered absentmindedly that it was a lot quieter than usual. Not that the center of the Elders was ever really high-spirited and frolicsome, but it very even more guarded and quiet than it usually was. Various members of the Elders could be seen hurrying around rapidly while they hugged the edges of the hallways, eventually finding their way down a flight of stairs that neither Kitty nor Mignonne had ever been ventured down. Taylor blanched slightly when he saw where they were heading, making Kitty wonder if perhaps had been down this staircase, and why did he suddenly look so disturbed about it? Aris, Pytel, and Taleka, who'd been working with Taylor, were usually waiting in the front hallway for the three of them, but they were alarmingly absent today, and the three Oracles felt pretty lost as they continued down the hall. *Get it together, Mignonne*, Mignonne thought to herself, *it's not like it's your first time here, stop being such a wuss*. She couldn't help being nervous though. Something morbid seemed to be hanging in the air in here. Kitty also was having some very unpleasant thoughts about this situation and felt even more trapped than she normally did in closed in indoor spaces, the darkness of the hall seeming to press in on her with increasing aggressive movement. When they reached the end of the hallway, where the steps going down were located, with wide eyes Taylor turned to Kitty and Mignonne, whispering, "This isn't good, guys."

Not bothering to speak in a hushed voice, Mignonne tried to hide her nerves as she turned to Taylor and met his gaze defiantly. "How the hell do you know, Taylor? Have you ever been downstairs?" She posed this question as if daring Taylor to reveal if he knew anything about what was happening, or what was located down these stairs, since she and Kitty sure didn't! Responding to her thinly veiled criticism, Taylor bristled and squared his shoulders behind his back. "Why yes, Mignonne, it happens that I have been; they took me there before they dropped me off at the house with you two after my flight landed in Scotland. They obviously weren't expecting me so soon, and there's a large, dark conference room down there. And they put me through a string of tests while we were there. These tests were not in any way pleasant; for one they brought a bucket of water to the table and plunged my head in it while two of them held me down. I fought, but I couldn't shake them off, and I almost passed out from lack of oxygen before instinct kicked in and I somehow managed to move the water away from my head and out over the edges of the basin. They seemed really tickled that I did this, and then spun some story about how they *didn't really* try to drown me; they were just testing my inborn abilities with water, since I was so evidently eager to join them and learn about my abilities. I would've walked out then, but while I was fuming upstairs Taleka came and sat with me. She said that she was sorry about that, the other Elders were suspicious and didn't trust her abilities to distinguish a true Oracle, particularly one so overzealous as I seemed to be. She begged me not to leave, saying that the other Elders would really punish her failure to retain one of the Oracles who had been placed in her care. She described some really old-school punishment methods that would probably happen to her if I left. So, I stayed." Kitty and Mignonne looked at each other in horror after Taylor told his story, it finally dawning on them that maybe the Elders were not a peaceful group of grandparents desperately seeking their grandchildren. Seeking, yes, but maybe they were not really good after all?

Hearing Taylor's account of what had happened his first night here raised so many new questions in Mignonne's and Kitty's minds. And it left Mignonne sorry that she'd snapped at him and Kitty frantically wondering why she and Mignonne hadn't been subjected to this initial treatment. Was it because they were not seen as much of a threat because they were *girls*? Even this thought made her narrow her eyes in anger, huffing with indignation and contemplating how best to prove to the Elders that even *girls* could give them a run for their money! As she was fuming, they heard a door open down the stairs, and Omage ran and mounted the stairs rapidly, stopping short in front of the three breathing heavily, desperately trying to catch his breath so that he could speak. Panting, he looked up at them and said with a watery determination to be cheerful, "Oh good morning, my dear Oracles! Fancy seeing you three here." The chuckle accompanying this greeting sounded off to Mignonne, and it left her wondering, what was Omage hiding? Kitty was still staring at him with defiance as he put his hands on her and Mignonne's shoulders, steering the three of them into an empty room that happened to be pretty closely adjacent to where they were standing. "The Elders didn't mean for our session to run so long as to have the three of you arrive before it was completed; I do apologize for that," were Omage's rushed words as he ushered them into the room, motioning to a few rickety seats located around a cheap looking table; obviously this room wasn't used much. Taylor remained standing rebelliously at the doorway, glaring at Omage as if daring him to make any move that could even be supposed as belligerent. Seeing Taylor's hostile expression, Omage smiled sheepishly and sighed before he began to explain to three of them what the turmoil in the center this morning was about.

Omage stood in front of the fireplace in the room, facing away from Taylor, Kitty, and Mignonne when he finally began speaking, his voice dragging as if he was again feeling a little reluctant. "My dear friends, I want to express my deepest apologies for everything that is going on here this morning. The Elders have been involved in a discussion pertaining to how best to approach you three with this development." "Well, you won't know until you try, will ya?" Taylor said rebelliously, making and holding eye contact with Omage, who had turned to face them. Omage again smiled sheepishly and shook his head, but seemed determined not to be distracted from telling them what it was clearly his mission to say. Omage looked down before he began, his eyes shifting warily in a manner quite unlike his usually cool and impartial demeanor. "The Elders have been attempting to bring over here the oracle of ether, but he seems reluctant and suspicious, not aided I am sure by the fact that his brother has been talking incessantly about the unbelievable nature of the claim of the existence and presence of the Oracles." Omage sighed, rubbed his fingers against his temples, and continued: "Now, I'm not pretending to claim that he is potentially in control of one of the rarest and unconsciously sought after elements is in any way that is either practical or logistically believable, but I was hoping that to utilize the pattern of individuals who maintain as much as you three have, management of this situation. I was hoping that we would continue to find people willing to accept, at first, by some degree of faith the complexity of this situation and their part in it. At any rate, the Elders have thus far been unsuccessful in our abilities to convince this young gentleman otherwise than he is determined to believe, and we feel that the approaching storm, the very reason we are attempting to gather and train all of you, warrants more decisive action on our part." Omage smiled a little malevolently at this for one brief instant, but immediately seemed to regain control of himself and put a blank expression back on his face. Kitty and Mignonne were a little startled by this sudden shift in how Omage was behaving and talking, and a flash of real fear crossed their minds. Mignonne felt quite surprised by this sudden shift in Omage, and asked herself what they did in fact really *know* about this person or his 'order of the Elders.' Kitty too felt the atmosphere in the room shift incredibly quickly back and forth depending on Omage's spirit, and someone who had such control of such a great expanse of a room made her automatically pretty wary. Omage was not in the least bothered by their reactions or their thinly veiled fears and worries, and he finally sat down to deliver what he thought might become quite a long story.

Omage spotted several new people, fellow members of the Elders, Kitty judged by their dress and their formality in entering the room, hands folded in front of their chests as they entered the small unused room in an extremely orderly single file line. There were only about six of them plus Omage, but Mignonne felt like she had in grade school when the principal and all of the teachers gathered together to make an announcement. In fact, she felt a little worried just as she had then that definitely the student body, maybe her in particular, was in trouble for some kind of action that warranted all of the authority figures to be present for some sort of action. Almost instinctively she began racking her brains over what she could possibly have done that might a problem but catching herself doing this she shrugged and forced herself to calm down. After all, what was really scary about a room full of men and women wearing bizarre clothes and being quiet? She was unable to continue this reverie, however, because almost immediately Omage stepped forward with a relieved expression on his face. "The Elders are gathering," Omage and the other Elders began intoning softly. "We are gathering, and we have a request." The Elders seemed to breathe out simultaneously, and Kitty and Mignonne wondered about their synchronicity, and they exchanged worried glances, wondering what kind of new age cult they might have gotten mixed into. Aris and Pytel were present, but it was another Elder (possibly Taylor's instructor?), an attractive African woman, who stepped forward and quite ceremonially handed a rolled up piece of paper to

Omage. Omage inclined his head to the other Elder, and then turned to look at Mignonne, Kitty, and Taylor. "My three Oracles," he began, "let us begin, as we have much to discuss.

"One of our contacts in Egypt, who also has attempted to reason with the Oracle of Ether and his family, has kept on systematically attempting to break down this Oracle's resistance to the news regarding his nature and has in fact made more progress than the rest of us here," Omage motioned at the other Elders behind him. "This woman, a dedicated and highly skilled priestess of one of the temples of existence in the material world, has told us that this young man is insisting that he meet the other, as he called it, 'supposed Oracles' before he will believe. Apparently, he doubts, though I am not sure how that could be. We have been tracking him all of his life for even longer than we have you three, and for his whole existence he has manifested his abilities and used them to unconsciously manipulate and control whatever room he finds himself in. For the fact that he has such an imposing and haughty nature he is not extremely popular, as I am sure that you can believe." Omage attempted to smile sheepishly, but finding himself incapable of doing so effectively he gave up and began addressing them more in the manner in which a military sergeant might address his troops; he squared his shoulders back, folded his arms behind his back, and stood straight and tall and he very nearly barked out. "Be that as it may, he has become something of a loner, and seems to depend on the opinion of his brother for everything, even though this is his half-brother and he himself is several years older than this man. What I am going to ask of the three of you is that you go to visit this gentleman, tell him, *show him*, of the truth of his being an oracle, and do *whatever is necessary* in order to bring him back here."

At this junction, Omage handed Kitty the folded up paper, seeming to deem her perpetually as the most rational of the three (*why the hell would he think that?* Kitty found herself asking mentally again); "I have brought the three of you here so that you might all know in detail this situation, but I and the other Elders have been ruminating and consulting the heavens and we feel that what needs to be done will be the most effective if Kitty and Mignonne alone go to him." Taylor immediately began to sputter in indignation, but Omage held up a hand to silence him and continued marching on in his monologue; "You, my esteemed Water Oracle, have had even less training in your gifts than Mignonne or Kitty have, and while your progress is commendable," Omage inclined his head so that Taylor would know he was being paid a compliment, "I and the other Elders just do not feel that you are convinced enough of your own abilities to be able to convince someone else of their own unique gifts." Here again Omage smiled, *almost saucily?* Mignonne thought, before he continued addressing them. "And in addition to that problem, it is commonly known that for an aggressive male, like the brother, females are much better at being non-threatening and convincing." "Hold up, hold up," a quite outraged Mignonne suddenly burst out, "We're also being sent to speak to this dude because we're *girls*, and we're *non-threatening?* I take serious offense at that, Mr. Elder." Mignonne had narrowed her eyes and her breathing had accelerated and seeming very willing to jump on this band wagon Kitty also exclaimed "Yeah!" and also tried to square her shoulders, her mind revisiting countless women's rights campaigns that she had participated in with her mother. Omage saw that this was not going to go over well as a joke of any kind, and he immediately revised his tactics. "Mignonne, Kitty, you have my apologies. I only meant to pay tribute to the physiological truth that in a great deal of instances a woman's presence can be calming." Omage waved both hands across his chest and seeming rather flustered sighed and continued. "If we are all able to be calm and speak rationally, I will continue to tell you details about this oracle."

Omage continued, "I have gathered you here today with some of my fellow Elders in order to tell you about the circumstances that we find ourselves within when dealing with the Ether Oracle. He is young, though several years older than any of you, and he has been manifesting all of his life with abilities which are in conjunction with his gifts as an Oracle, perhaps even more so than you three. His abilities, however, are less obviously seen. He is in denial, and his family is not being of any help in convincing him otherwise, and so he is in need to more desperate action in order to be convinced regarding his nature. You, Mignonne, and you, Kitty, may not be able to see it, but the two of you have been making outstanding progress in your training with your particular elements, and I believe that simply seeing the two of you, hopefully with you two telling him of our veracity, will be decisive in not only convincing him that he is indeed one of you Oracles, but that the Elders are not a malevolent enemy. The scroll which I have handed to our Earth Oracle contains pertinent details regarding this person and some jots about his history, just so that the two of you will be able to stay abreast of any cultural discrepancies which you might come across when dealing with him. Please, review this information and let us know by tomorrow if you two would be willing to go and simply talk with this young man. The Elders will provide transportation and, if necessary, lodging, though I do not believe that this will be required, judging from our good relations with the priestesses located near this place." At this, Omage seemed to reach the end of his discourse, and he and the other Elders who were present in the room bowed to the three and proceeded to leave the room just as orderly as they had entered. Omage did stop at the doorway, though, and turned to look at the three of them. "Kitty, Mignonne, the Elders have discussed it and we believe that something of this magnitude which is in need of answer so quickly warrants us giving the two of you the day today to review this scroll and talk amongst yourselves, letting us know your decision as soon as possible, if you should so please. Taylor though, we also feel that you cannot afford to lose any day of training as late coming to this situation as you were." This sounded to Mignonne, Kitty, and by the looks of it, Taylor, to be quite rude and presumptuous; why was Taylor being punished just because he was a little late to the game!? Not his fault, after all! After a moment though, Taylor turned to the girls and smiled like there was something really going on in his head. "Go ladies, go without worry; *the Elders* have no idea how especially *cooperative* I'm going to be today during my *training.*" Taylor then turned and strode out of the room, leaving Kitty and Mignonne to smile questioningly and then to start laughing before they left, ruminating about whatever hijinks Taylor had planned as punishment to the Elders for their disrespect and general smarminess to him.

Never ones to say no to a free day off, Mignonne and Kitty left the building quickly, as if worrying that if they gave the Elders too much time to think about it then their day off would be revoked; this really made them both feel like they were still in high school, yes. Kitty did wonder once they approached the doorway leading outside how she they were going to get back to their house, but this question was answered almost immediately; Grace, one of their other typical drivers among the Elders, was waiting in front of the car that had picked them up that morning, and she hurried to get in the drivers' seat while Kitty and Mignonne approached and then got into the car themselves. Like most of their drivers (they couldn't really shake giving these people this title), Grace said little, and though Kitty and Mignonne eyed each other nervously they said nothing until they were back home and alone in their house. Kitty had been holding the document quite stiffly without realizing this, and when they got in she realized this and she attempted to unlock her fingers from around the scroll; while she flexed and massaged her hand a little, Mignonne had proceeded to make good on the day off, kicked off her shoes, and gone into the kitchen to make more coffee (she did have such a fondness for what she termed her own version of 'black gold'). Eventually, cup in hand, she went and sat at the kitchen table with Kitty, who was poring over the scroll. "So, Kit-Kat, what's it say?" Mignonne sang out; she always tried to add some blitheness to any potentially bad situation. "Well, Miggy, this scroll doesn't say a lot, but from what I'm understanding this guy's name is Arkite Iry-Pat (how weird is that name? Or is that a family title?), and he is twenty-four years old. Apparently he and his brother live in the family home, which is a Nubian-looking mansion with their parents, who seem kind of important in the local community. It says he enjoys racing horses across the desert, enjoying a mulled glass of wine, and retreating into solitude in the peace of the desert night. How much like a weird dating profile does that sound, jeez." Kitty felt kind of irritated as she tossed the scroll down, leaving it for Mignonne to pick up and peruse.

After spending a good deal of time looking over the scroll herself, Mignonne finally put it back on the table and prepared to get down to the pertinent question. "So, Kitty, this guy and his whole family sound weird, and I'm a little nervous about going to Egypt, what with all the political/religious unrest that seems to happen there. But if what this page is telling us is true, the Elders just want us to go and talk to this guy; I have no intention of convincing anyone of anything, but if they'll pay for us to go to Egypt and talk to this dude then I don't see why not, judging from all the other strange things that we have done at their behest. 'Sides," Mignonne intoned, "we've always wanted to travel, right?" Kitty seem unamused by Mignonne and stood up and started pacing in the kitchen. "Egypt is a much scarier place to go than Scotland, if we're thinking about safety, and I'm not sure that if this guy is so unconvinced that he's an Oracle that we should go and try to convince him otherwise, leading to a drastic up-heaval of his life? I mean, freedom of thought, right? If he wants to stay at home with his brother, who seems kind of angsty, should we go and try to make him come here?" Ceding that these questions were valid and worth deliberating over, Mignonne jotted down a couple of notes to ask the Elders, and she and Kitty decided to stop going through this painful deliberation, at least for the rest of this day; they figured that they would hash everything out with Omage tomorrow.

Chapter 15

Hijr

The next morning was a Saturday, and the girls generally did not have training on Saturdays, but one of the Elders (Kitty thought her name was Chloe?), had told them that the car would come to pick them up a little after 8:00. Mignonne suspected that this was because Omage and company had already purchased plane tickets for the two of them for a flight that would be leaving pretty early. At any rate, Kitty and Mignonne were up early getting ready for the day, Kitty endlessly chipper and Mignonne groggy; Mignonne fervently hoped that wherever they were going would have strong, robust coffee. As they waited out on their front lawn, with Mignonne drowsing on the steps and Kitty carefully examining her garden, they were both surprised to see Taylor come outside and join them. He wore a resigned look as he leaned against the bannister that was flanking the steps, and he seemed determined as he told them to be careful, and not to put a great deal of trust in the safety that the Elders were so willing to forego by sending them out presumably alone to Egypt. Before Mignonne could ask what he thought the dangers might be (anything other than the normal travel dangers, like pickpocketing?)

a black sedan pulled up and whisked Kitty and Mignonne away. And when it turned away from how they normally got to the training center, Mignonne felt her heart start racing as she leaned forward in her seat. She got even more nervous when the driver did not respond to her question about where they were going, and she sank back into her seat and exchanged a worried look with Kitty. Kitty was about to demand to know where they were going when the car pulled directly into a small private airport and stopped in front of Omage, who was wringing his hands and was clearly waiting for their arrival.

Kitty wrenched her door open as soon as the car stopped, leaving Mignonne to try to grab both of their bags upon exiting (they hadn't been sure what to pack, not knowing how long they were staying, but they'd both brought only two outfits, and if they were staying longer they fervently hoped that they'd be able to find a laundry mat). By this point Kitty had worked herself into a tizzy and she flew at Omage; why had they been taken directly to an airport? And a run-down airport at that!? Kitty hadn't quite outgrown being a teenage drama queen, but then again neither had Mignonne. What kind of game did the Elders think they were playing, that Mignonne and Kitty would be always ready to be taken to new places at the whim of the Elders without *the slightest hint at what would happen there*? They weren't exactly in Scotland with the Order long term for their health, for Pete's sake! Omage looked at Kitty and at the struggling to awaken Mignonne like he was a little sorry at first, but at Kitty's tirade his face clouded over, and he stopped treating them like anything except deluded children. "Ladies," he stated in a very clipped tone, "I thought it was agreed upon when you began working with the Elders that we are at liberty to utilize you and your abilities to whatever extent that we so choose? Or did the two of you fool yourselves into thinking that this fully funded trip to Scotland would come completely without the two of you paying or helping us? If so I do apologize, and please, allow me to set the record straight, so to speak." Omage smiled malevolently as he finished saying this, and he forcefully grabbed Kitty's arm and the bags that Mignonne was carrying (regardless that she was still holding them and didn't let go) as he walked them to a dilapidated seat outside the small, poorly kept building. Once they were standing in front of the seat, neither of them being really inclined to sit, they realized that Omage not only had them in an extremely compromising situation, with them only knowing the slightest details about what they'd be doing. Omage shortly told them that a private jet would be arriving soon and that they were to get on this plane and let it take them to Egypt, where the contact that Omage had spoken of would meet them and direct them as to what the day would bring. As he handed them both an envelope, his eyes narrowed. "These envelopes contain directives once you have reached the airport; our source of communication has been the priestess of the hijr, someone that I feel sure will explain everything concerning what is to be expected of the two of you." As he stopped talking a small rather rickety little plane began to land on the tarmac nearby, and Mignonne and Kitty found their baggage being tossed into it and themselves being shoved quickly into seats where they were buckled up *(as if we were children? they both thought rather petulantly)*, and shortly enough Omage and the Scottish countryside started to recede into the distance. They were unable to really talk because of the close proximity of the pilot who they had not heard speaking in anything other than Arabic over his radio, but they were extremely suspicious of him and didn't dare discount his possible ability to speak English. The roar of the engine also contributed to their silence, Mignonne thought, smiling ruefully.

After an extremely unpleasant flight, owing to the cramped space and the very fact that a complete stranger was flying them over the ocean in a tiny jet that they weren't entirely sure wouldn't capsize into the ocean; many of the waves looked bigger than the plane, and a few came what seemed to be dangerously close to the edges of the jet. Kitty had to fight nausea caused by the swooping plane as well as worry that the next big wave would take it out *(weren't they flying too close to the water, after all?)* and Mignonne, who was feeling concerns about both of these things but still managed to be really irritated about the whole situation despite her best efforts, tucked her legs into her chest and tried not to look out the window. The plane might have been tiny and fragile, but the little plane made good time over the Atlantic, and in about six hours they were landing on a small flight pad located amidst sand and palm trees, with the shadows from the sun showing them that it was only slightly later than it would be if they were still in Scotland. Once the plane touched down, Kitty and Mignonne grabbed their suitcases out of the back of the plane and thankfully tumbled out, it seemed immediately onto the sand, which never seemed to end around them but gave the impression of a kind of still, beige sea.

Mignonne looked pensively about her, but nothing and no one was apparent apart from the sand dunes; in desperation she looked at Kitty, her eyes wild as she contemplated what new situation they had gotten themselves into. When she turned to rap on the plane window to try and ask the pilot something (*he might speak English, right?* she thought to herself), she and Kitty heard the plane motor turn on she instinctively jerked back, pulling Kitty farther back into the endless sand with her. Even though it lacked a long runway to take off of, apparently the tiny jet had a more powerful engine than they had first thought, and it seemed to take off without any trouble practically from a stationary position, much they'd seen a helicopter do once or twice in their lives. As Kitty and Mignonne shielded their faces from the sand that was kicked up around them, Mignonne turned to her friend, blurting out of desperation, "Kitty! Where are we? Who's coming to get us? Are we going to die in the desert!?" Kitty shared Mignonne's concerns, but at least some vestige of her usually calm demeanor remained, and though she was actually trembling a little out of fear, her usual drama defense mechanism not even working. She met Mignonne's eyes valiantly and forced herself to give a tremulous watery smile, thinking that it really couldn't get a lot worse (she hoped). Mignonne occupied herself by pacing in about a twenty-foot circle around them, searching for anything is this forsaken place that would make any kind of sense to her, grasping at straws for comfort, or at least assurance. Suddenly, she spotted a figure that seemed to materialize about fifty yards from them; at first she wasn't sure if this was a mirage, though; *was the desert already starting to get to her?* she worried. Mignonne's heart started racing and it wasn't until Kitty also seemed to spot this figure making their way towards them that Mignonne felt more assured. Kitty herself was grasping Mignonne's arm and feeling nauseated again.

Because Kitty obviously also saw this person, Mignonne felt reassured, but as the outline in the desert became clearer, it was Kitty who eventually called out in a desperate voice, more out of panic than bravery, but she reassured herself, if her panic caused action was it really not a form of bravery? "Hey! You there! Can you speak English?" came Kitty's voice calling across the short distance between them and the woman (yes, they saw that she was a woman now, though extremely oddly dressed). The approaching woman wasn't wearing anything that Kitty or Mignonne recognized from anywhere; she wasn't dressed like anybody that they had previously come into contact with, but was wearing a pair of dark blue baggy capri pants, belted by a tan colored sash, and a reddish brown tube top; large audacious looking jewelry also decorated her, with a wide silver bracelet around both wrists, chunky bronze colored earrings reaching down her neck almost to her shoulders, and a large bronze, gold, and silver necklace adorning her throat and dropping down onto her chest. A large ruby was at the heart of her necklace, and Kitty found herself momentarily preoccupied by watching what seemed like infinite glimmer exuding from the stone. Once the lady got closer to them, Mignonne also noticed that alongside her chunky jewelry she sported tattoos on her right cheek, her right shoulder/upper arm, and along the right side of her stomach. These markings looked more akin to hieroglyphics than any tattoo that Mignonne remembered seeing, and the dark red of the tattoos contrasted her own bronze skin and her dark pants strikingly. She looked altogether wild to the girls, but as she approached them, apparently giving them a quick once over with her sharp, dark brown eyes, her gaze softened and she stopped about five feet away from them, clasping her hands together in front of her chest and making a quick bow of greeting. "Earth. Air," she intoned, "I am honored to meet the two of you. My name is Ishept, and I am the acquaintance of whom Omage surely spoke. While the order of the moon goddess, of which I am a part, generally does not associate with other orders like the Elders, we have joined the Elders in seeking and finding the Oracles, for the great good of all the world. Please, accompany me and I will escort you two into our own sacred place."

Ishept led a dumbfounded Mignonne and Kitty about sixty feet away along the sand, and as they were continually sinking into it and feeling it in the shoes, Kitty (more relieved, now that another human had appeared), wondered disgruntledly how far they were going to have to trek across the endless desert; granted, it was really good resistance training, but neither she nor Mignonne were wearing anything really suited to trekking across the desert. Of course, Ishept didn't appear to be either, but she moved with confidence and grace, indicating that this was her home with which she was very familiar. Moving along the continually shifting sand with ease while Mignonne and Kitty shuffled along behind her, Ishept quickly approached and then stopped at a stone marker protruding from a sand dune, a miniature black obelisk with silver markings on it that was standing only about three feet tall, maybe two feet wide? Wondering what in the world was happening, Mignonne looked furtively around for any signs of human habitation, but before she could really become worried over seeing nothing, Ishept turned three portions of the top of the obelisk, which moved surprisingly easily, aligning three of the same symbols. She then stepped backwards and lo and behold, the obelisk shifted backwards to reveal a small hole into the ground, with worn stairs leading down. Ishept motioned for Kitty and Mignonne to enter the rather dark passageway first and thinking that she and Mignonne were too far into this to chicken out now, Kitty screwed up her courage and moved in front of the entrance. Mignonne followed behind her, and together they started making their way slowly down the stairs, fervently hoping that it would continue to be lighted the further that they went down away from the desert sun.

Yes, it turned out that there were small torches along the staircase that became quite obvious when Ishept turned behind herself and clicked a mechanism to bring the tiny obelisk marker back over the entranceway. The lights were really quite bright once the sun was no longer shining down into the sand ringed passage, and the staircase was not long before they found themselves in a sort of hallway made completely of stone. Not knowing where to go or what to do, Mignonne and Kitty shifted uncomfortably back and forth, but somehow a feeling of calm displaced their fear, at least for a little while. The very air in this place seemed to hum with a sort of peace. Mignonne still wasn't sure what was happening or that they were not in real and imminent danger, but a calmness of resignation seemed to settle on her as she stood looking around and seeing not much besides the stone walls, floor, and ceiling. Darkness was along was along one passageway, but to the girls' relief Ishept led them along another walkway that was in fact lit, and into a large cavern which seemed brighter than it should be, even accounting for the small torches. It was lit only with about four torches, but the moonstones which adorned all of the walls and ceiling, and decorated an elaborate altar, reflected the light and seemed to form tiny balls of illumination from their core that shone out across all of the stone walls. The room was made entirely of what looked like granite, though this was a fact that was easily overlooked as any person in question gazed intently into the heart of the moonstones, which seemed to draw the viewer in with an irresistible power and allow them to drown in the eternity that is God. Mignonne especially felt the urge to dive into these depths promised by the stones, and she did not care very much if she resurfaced; something in the stones she felt vibrating in her bones and promising entrance into a world of darkness that was not dark, but filled with white light, into a sea that would not require her to breathe. She was moving towards the altar, caught in this fantasy, when Kitty grabbed her arm and looked at her questioningly. This jolt back into reality made Mignonne shake her head as if to clear the cobwebs and she re-centered her gaze on Ishept, who was smiling furtively at her and shaking her head, struggling not to laugh.

Finally, after they had passed what could have possibly been a bizarre entrance ritual of some sort, Ishept sat down on one of the stone steps and motioned for the two to join her. She smoothed her baggy pants out and then swept her arms through the air, apparently not seeing or not choosing to see Mignonne and Kitty staring at her and wondering if she might be a crazy person. "The Elder Omage told me the names that the two of you go by in this realm of consciousness, but I think it more appropriate to address the two of you as the elements that you have command over, for this is your true being. I and the others in the service of the moon goddess Eie-ep-son are quite thrilled that in our lifetime the Oracles have returned and manifested into this physical realm. Imagine how even more thrilled we were to find that one of the other Oracles is here, in Egypt." Ishept smiled happily when giving this news, but her happiness seemed to drop from her face immediately as she continued. "Sadly though, this Oracle of the Ether, perhaps the most powerful and spiritually oriented of the five of you, has rejected his destiny and has retreated into hiding. Undoubtedly, Omage has told the both of you that he is being guarded jealously by his brother, who apparently does not understand that without the proper training his brother will be the missing portion of a vast and tremendously powerful chain. The fate of this entire generation could be in question should he not change his thinking. This oracle, Arkite is the name that he goes by, wishes to hide from the truth of his nature, but I am hopeful along with Omage and the Elders that with help from the two of you Arkite will come to see the beauty of his gift. It is a quite obvious act of grace that the two of you have embraced your destinies so readily, eagerly, even from what I have heard, and seeing the two of you I am even more confident in your ability to help Arkite. But the first challenge in this endeavor will be finding him," Ishept added gravely. "He is quite the recluse, retreating often into the vast and endless desert, where it is difficult even for us to track him, and at other times he chooses to hide in the enormity of his father's estate. So, he is going to be quite difficult to make any contact with, and then once you have found him, he must be convinced to return with you two. But I am hopeful that he will be drawn to the two of you in a way that he is not able to understand, and so will come out of hiding. But no matter, what will be has already been written into the endless dance of the heavens, and we are all merely dancers trying to keep rhythm with it. I know that this was a great deal to hear, so immediately following your arrival especially, and so I will leave the two of you now, and Indrineela, one of my fellow priestesses, will show the two of you where you will be sleeping." At this pronouncement Ishept rose from her seat and left the room in a fluid motion, quite before a flabbergasted Kitty and Mignonne could think of any questions to ask or to wonder out loud where they might be spending the night. Another priestess, still sporting audacious jewelry and gemstones but also with a hood pulled up loosely over her head, materialized in the chamber seemingly out of thin air. "Greetings, Those Who See the Heart of the World. I am Indrineela, and I know that the two of you must be weary from your travels. Please, allow me to lead you to your chambers." At this she turned away from Kitty and Mignonne and started walking briskly towards a hallway to the left of them, leaving them to scramble to their feet and trot after her, not much wanting to be left alone in the huge, cavernous chamber of stone.

Chapter 16

Many Findings and Goings

Once Indrineela had deposited Kitty and Mignonne in a thankfully not cavernous or intimidating small bed chamber located off one of the hallways, Mignonne gave her surroundings a quick survey before she turned to Kitty with relief in her eyes. "Oh, Kitty. I was so scared for a while, but Ishept and Indrineela seem cool, right? Weird yes, but nice enough?" Her voice was almost pleading for reassurance. Kitty met Mignonne's gaze as she was depositing her belongings on the lower part of a bunk bed which was carved quite naturally out of a stone wall; she hoped the mattress would be sufficient. Kitty often slept outside among the plants and earth of her garden back home, but she didn't think that stone would feel quite the same. "Yeah, Miggy, it seems okay. For now. I think we've accidentally stumbled across some of my mom's existential club." Kitty smiled widely at this, and then speculated, "I wonder when or if they're gonna feed us, or if they exist on moonbeams or something." She shook her head at this and eagerly stretched out over her bed. Mignonne climbed the wall which had been engraved with steps and fell back on the higher bed pallet, laughing at Kitty's foolishness but then secretly wondering, what if she was right!? This was the last thing that she thought before her travel fatigue caught up to her and she almost instantly fell asleep on what felt quite like she thought a thin straw mat would, lulled by the security and stability of the stone surrounding her. She and Kitty were both awakened about an hour later by Indrineela, who slid back the sliding stone door and entered the little room bearing a tray of food that had been apparently made after Kitty's vegetarian soul; she bowed and apologized for waking them, but Mignonne thought that it was just as well. Her biological clock told her that it was getting late in the evening and she knew that if she had slept any longer sleep tonight would be entirely out of the question. Having enjoyed many vegetarian dinners with Kitty and Ms. Stone, Mignonne liked partaking of her meal alongside a very ravenous Kitty, who was so excited over the fare that she was eating more and faster than she normally did. Feeling rested and refreshed from her nap and meal, Kitty pushed the tray away from her and then sat back on her bed, where she was soon joined for a chat by Mignonne (the room was so tiny that it really had no other seating space). "So Miggy, what do you think we'll do be scheduled to do tomorrow?" Kitty asked rather unintentionally plaintively. Mignonne met Kitty's eyes and took a deep breath, preparing to begin what promised to be a rather long conversation until they both got tired again and returned to sleep.

The next morning (they assumed it was morning, anyway), Indrineela, who'd apparently been tasked with being their guide, appeared at their door again. She led a groggy Kitty and Mignonne to what thankfully was a lot like a bathroom made completely of granite and limestone with small white accent stones everywhere, and the two gratefully got cleaned up, washing travel sweat and sand off of themselves. "Indrineela?" Kitty queried, "Where do you guys get the running water down here? Aren't we pretty far beneath a desert with no city water near?" Indrineela seemed happy that Kitty had asked and launched into a long explanation about how in this part of the world there was water to be found everywhere, and the priestesses were expert at coaxing this hidden underground water into their kitchen and bathrooms, using quite ancient designs within the stone to guide the water into these places. Mignonne shook her head at the ingenuity that the priestesses had developed so that they could exist in the desert, and Kitty looked at Indrineela with eyes full of respect and admiration. After the girls had cleaned up, using this fabulous underground water and a bar of tallow soap made from candle wax, Indrineela nervously asked them if they would be interested in joining the priestesses for breakfast. Eager to learn more about this hidden order and other incredible methods that they had found to exist in this environment (like how did they get food?), Kitty and Mignonne both nodded and briskly followed Indrineela down a long and twisting stone walkway and into another immense room, this time filled with stone tables and accompanying benches. Once they were seated they discussed with Ishept exactly what she thought the best plan of at least looking for Arkite would be, since that was supposed to be their reason for being here; forget convincing him of anything for right now. Ishept pondered as she ate from her bowl of quinoa; while she was thinking, Kitty and Mignonne were nervously trying to avoid the eager eyes of the other ten priestesses, who apparently were amazed to see the Oracles, or perhaps they just never had visitors. Not knowing quite what to do, they were both relieved when Ishept cleared her throat and began talking.

"I can show you two how to get to where in the city Arkie generally is; let's hope that he is not somewhere in his prodigious family holdings, where he would be inaccessible — you should see the guards they have posted at all entrances, they are quite opposed to random visitors — but that he is instead located somewhere more open to the public. We are quite near the city of Thebes, and if he is somewhere there that would help, though it might still be difficult to find him. Let us pray that he is not difficult to find wherever it happens that he is." At this pronouncement, Ishept told both girls that camels had been prepared, should they care to ride, adding before Mignonne's panic at a solo trip on a camel took over her, that they would be ac-companied by expert Nomadic guides, who were quite necessary when someone was new to the desert. Mignonne felt relief at this until she and Kitty climbed the staircase back into the open desert and emerged into a bright day, finding two of what they assumed were Nomads holding the leashes on two camels who had blankets on their backs. Seeing these tremendous beasts who looked quite a great deal bigger than ye olde horse, Mignonne was suddenly struck by not so much the mere size of the camel, but rather by the intelligence that it looked at her with, inviting her to climb aboard its back and travel with this native guide through the sea of sand. Passing a grin to Kitty, Mignonne moved towards her camel; the beast lay down in an accom-modating way so that she could climb on, she did so without hesita-tion. Kitty also mounted her camel, who was not so nice as to lay down but who did not protest as one of the Nomad's helped Kitty to mount up. The ride to Thebes took only about half an hour, and both girls were actually enjoying greatly their respective camel rides that the time passed quickly. Mignonne and Kitty were each reluctant to dismount their camels once they reached the city of Thebes, but they did so, with their guide promising in broken English to return to the place where the girls had been dropped about midday to take them back to the temple. Not knowing what else to do, Kitty and Mignonne began wandering through a nearby outdoor marketplace, not daring to leave the public eye unaccompanied in a foreign land.

Thebes was a huge city, and the girls quickly lost any hope of finding this so-called Arkite; Thebes was simply too big for them to come up with any conceivable way to explore thoroughly in one day anyway and feeling rather miffed that Ishept and the other pries-tesses hadn't given them any better advice Mignonne and Kitty re-solved to not occupy themselves with looking but rather to enjoy themselves in this new and different city. They explored the market, and each had a baked sweet potato bought from a vendor near one of the fountains. And as they sat on the edge of the fountain, they contemplated what to do next. Kitty really wanted to explore the immense library that was located near the marketplace, and while Mignonne's enthusiasm was not as great as Kitty's about this, she agreed to join her friend in going here. Kitty was soon so captivated by the myriad papyrus scrolls that were in the library alongside more normal and modern books that she didn't really notice when Mignonne sat down and prepared to wait.

As Kitty eagerly scurried through the library, she found herself not so much interested in the small section of regular books in English (one of which Mignonne had grabbed and was attempting to become absorbed in, without great success), as the vast shelves of papyrus scrolls, which though newly made seemed to hark back thousands of years through the enormity of history and speak of their place in the Egyptian court and lifestyle. She tentatively grabbed one of the scrolls off the shelf, unfurling it carefully and then burying her head into the softly crackling material, not understanding the written words and hieroglyphics, but inhaling the scent which came off the papyrus and seemed to fill the entire library, a scent so strange and yet so familiar that she absorbed it like the attar of a choice rose. "I see you appreciate the depths of meaning found in a papyrus scroll," came a voice behind Kitty, and she started out of surprise. The young man who was behind her as she turned to face him (feeling a very weird electric jolt go through her body, leaving her tingling as she faced him) looked as if he was not quite sure what exactly to make of either her or his statement. It was quite obviously not in his nature to go around talking to strangers about random things like papyrus scrolls (and incidentally, Kitty wondered vaguely, was that his version of a nervous-guy pick-up line? This was a weird country so far). The man smiled awkwardly at Kitty and then seemed to lose his nerve, so he beat a hasty retreat out of the aisle and sort of hid behind another shelf.

Kitty stood with her feet planted in the spot she had been standing feeling disoriented and unable to move either her feet or her voice. This is how she stood when seconds later Mignonne came looking for her, her own skin feeling a crackling sensation, though not nearly as strong as Kitty's had been. As they looked at each other and exchanged furtive glances and words about what was going on another youngish looking man, this one wearing a more traditional ancient Egyptian robe, complete with arm bands and a golden headband hustled up to them. Mignonne was so astounded by his eccentric appearance that she let out a laugh even before the young person spoke. "Excuse me, ladies," he began in a heavily accented voice, "but I was wondering if either of you have seen my brother? He is quite thin and dressed much as I am?" Mignonne shook her head no while eyeing the person suspiciously (was it a common thing in Egypt for people just to walk up and ask random strangers questions, she wondered), but Kitty was already nodding. "Yeah, I think so. Some random guy just came up and said something to me before he disappeared that way." Kitty pointed back behind one of the aisles and the man flashed them a brilliant smile as he turned and began hurrying backwards towards where Kitty pointed. "Many thanks, lovely women," came his departing words and at the end of their aisle he paused, clasped his hands in front of his bare chest, and bowed. Kitty turned to face Mignonne, who was feeling pretty confused. In a slightly trembling voice, she quietly whispered to Mignonne, with wide eyes and even, Mignonne couldn't believe it, with a slight smile. "I think the guy who first came and talked to me might be who we're looking for, Miggy. I mean, Ishept and Omage told us that he was something of a recluse with an overbearing brother, right? What if that first guy was him? I mean, why else would he come and talk to me randomly and send shots of energy shooting up both of us?" Kitty was working herself up into a tizzy, and Mignonne felt that Kitty might need a little leveling out from the real world. "Calm down, Miss Kitty. I can think of a lot of reasons why a guy might approach a total stranger and make weird comments, and none of these involve 'mystical powers' or 'connection of destiny.' He might just have thought you were cute and then lost his nerve; it happens. Now come on, we're supposed to meet

Indrineela soon." At this, Mignonne turned and strode out of the library, feeling a little, a *very* little, miffed. How come random dudes didn't walk up to her in strange libraries and make bizarre statements!? The fact that this might be because her strong and confident personality scared a lot of people, but this didn't occur to her. *Oh well,* she shrugged once she was outside, *Kitty had always gotten more attention from the opposite sex than her,* and Kitty had such a sweet personality that she couldn't really blame them. Having a little time left, she and Kitty went and sat down on a bench on the edge of the marketplace, wishing they had been more successful in their mission (Mignonne couldn't help thinking of it like that), when they saw nervous guy approaching as if he'd been waiting for them to come outside.

As he approached, Kitty and Mignonne both sat forward and waited, with tiny tingling sensations and tremors passing through Kitty's body, at least. Kitty wondered if he'd be able to talk now and was actually relieved to have Mignonne with her (Miggy could make anyone talk). He stopped about five feet away from them and gazed at them as if he wasn't quite sure that they wouldn't immediately stand up and run at him. Growing tired of this waiting game, Mignonne sighed, sat forward, and snapped her fingers, demanding to know who he was, why he'd followed them, and what he hoped to gain for this. The young man seemed a little angry at Mignonne's abrupt questioning (he was obviously not used to being asked what he saw as personal questions, either by presumptuous Americans or anybody, really), but he only cleared his throat in response. His gaze darting between Mignonne and Kitty, he apparently decided that talking was necessary in this situation and he reluctantly cleared his throat and began, looking mostly at Kitty while he did so. "Please. Let's go inside the restaurant here and talk. It'll be less out in the open, and I'm quite sure that my beloved brother (he smiled a little sarcastically as he said this), won't, at least not immediately, look there." They figured that accompanying someone weirdo into a public restaurant at least wasn't any better or worse than their options, the girls stood and walked behind him. In the restaurant, he suddenly assumed a very lordly air, and he motioned to the staff members who were suddenly simpering and falling all over themselves as they followed in his direction and the three of them sat at a table in the middle of crowded dining room. Once seated he brusquely, but still with a quiet voice, ordered three teas; Mignonne was a trifle upset that he hadn't asked, but Kitty had a deep love of hot tea and simply smiled. Once their drinks arrived this random person sat back in his seat, and he began talking, quietly at first but gaining more volume and assurance as he went on.

"My name is Arkite Silveraii, and I am the first son of the distinguished Akhon Silveraii, of the ancient line descending from the goddess Mut," and he seemed to start feeling more at ease and cocked a smile as he said, "If it is your inclination to believe in ancient Egyptian mythology. Our family has always had direct involvement in affairs that were both economic and societal, and our father dreamed of one day having a son to whom he could pass this on. Unfortunately for him he had me first, and I have always been something of a perpetual disappoint to him; everything that he and my brother love, I detest. I hate being in the public eye, and I feel no desire to pursue anything having to do with government. I have always been more of a scholar than my younger half-brother, who is quite unlike me in every respect. I do not normally approach strange women at will at a place like the library and initiate conversations, but I felt quite drawn to you," he finished, staring in a rather sheepish fashion at Kitty. Tired of being ignored, Mignonne huffed, "Well, that's all very well and good, sir, and we do hope that one day Daddy loves you, but why talk to us? We're looking for someone, and we're supposed to meet our ride in about half an hour to go back." Arkite was again a trifle annoyed at Mignonne's abruptness, but he only sighed and sat forward in his chair. "Then I will get straight to the point. Did the two of you not feel any vibrations in your psyches when we first saw each other? I knew that was so to you, and it was so shocking," here he looked at Kitty, "that I couldn't help speaking. It was almost as if I felt a connection and vibration that goes deep into the very cogs and iron workings of existence, and I knew that I must speak to you. But I feel that I have overreached in this situation, and," Arkite stood up suddenly, leaving his nearly full tea on the table, "I will go, before my brother comes searching for me." He took a small ornately decorated leaflet out of his jacket and handed it to Mignonne. "This is an invitation for one of the annual gala get togethers that my father and brother throw; if you would like to speak to me more in depth, please attend. I will make sure that the security knows to expect the two of you." Here, he threw a couple bills on the table and strode out, leaving Kitty and Mignonne to clutch their rapidly cooling tea and wonder what it was that had just happened. Bells were going off in their heads, and they weren't exactly sure where the danger was, but they were certain that they were no longer in control of all the things that were happening; they could almost feel the gears of this life speed up as they continued to sit in the restaurant.

The nomads and the camels were not waiting on them in the desert at the appointed time, but once Kitty and Mignonne had gotten into the car that was sent for them from the temple (which was quite rusty from disuse) and been deposited back among Ishept and company, Mignonne showed the invitation written in words that she could not understand to Indrineela. The young priestess squealed in joy, exclaiming about how wonderful that they had already been invited to a Silveraii family party, and how excited she was for them! She had been sure that Arkite would be very willing to talk to them and find them, and perhaps he would be willing to make a new decision talking to them in such a relaxed setting as the party! Even though the party wasn't until the next night, Indrineela and then Ishept seemed to treat this invitation as the most wonderful news in the world, and both went off together exclaiming about the "magnetism of the Oracles" and "the need to come up with distinctive clothing." During this talk Kitty and Mignonne exchanged something of a worried look, and the two girls ducked into the room where they'd been getting away, fortunately, and avoiding being detained by any other rapturous priestess. It kind of was wearing on them to have to duck and cover like this; what had they gotten themselves into where this was a normal part of their daily lives now!? At any rate, they slipped away successfully, and shut and blocked off their door (it had no true lock, grrr, and easily could have been busted through); after they'd finished moving the dresser in front of the door, Mignonne looked at Kitty, her heart pounding as she breathed in deeply and prepared to talk.

Mignonne's words, when they came, were hushed; she still wasn't entirely sure that they weren't being watched or listened to, and the fact that she'd let this continue so far while she felt like that made her shake her head at herself in disbelief. It was entirely out of character for her to allow herself to get so swept up in something that she felt that she didn't have control of. Still, she looked at Kitty and her words came out softly and cautiously. "Kitty. I don't know how we've got ourselves into with all of this, and I'm really not okay with it. How stupid could I have been to let everything go off the deep end so truly and leave us helpless in a foreign country!? But I think we have to do something here. I mean, Omage and the Elders, Ishept, and the priesthood… these people are all trying to control us. *We* have the oracle abilities, and I'm sick of being tossed backwards and forth like a pinata! If we're so powerful, how is this happening? I don't know about you, but I'm 'bout to take control back of my life." After this rant, Mignonne breathed in deeply, shaking with adrenaline and excitement; now that she'd finally voiced her fears, she was ready to do whatever she could to stop them. Kitty, who had turned her back to Mignonne, moved once again to face forward towards her friend, and with serious eyes nodded her head. "Okay, Mignonne. I agree that we're in deep here, and something has to change before we get even further into this situation, where we get that we can't get out of. I don't know how we'll do it, but I say we run. Run and don't look back." Kitty breathed a sigh of relief once she'd said this, and she and Mignonne started immediately repacking their bags and quietly talking about what their options were.

The girls deliberated intently for a while over how best to escape; should they leave tonight in cover of darkness? Always a fan favorite for prison breaks they'd seen in books and movies. Should they run in the morning, while everyone was having breakfast? Kitty suggested that they stay the night, and even stay through the day tomorrow, and when they were shuttled to Arkite's family party the next night, they would use the fact that they wouldn't be surrounded by anybody who was responsible for their whereabouts and slip away, hopefully not being noticed in the unfamiliar crowds that were sure to be there. Mignonne still had, secreted away in her purse, a credit card that her parents had given her before she and Kitty left, telling her to use it for any emergencies that might occur; they apparently had been kind of equally nervous about their girls going overseas alone when they were barely adults. But they figured, everyone would take credit cards, right? Mignonne figured that she and Kitty could slip away from the party, into a cab, go to the airport, and buy the first available tickets home. Small details like how she and Kitty would be able to get a phone to call a cab with, or how they'd get a number for a cab company, they'd deal with when they came. High stress situations like this often impelled Mignonne to make these impulsive decisions. She would always, always rather dash madly into something and hope for the best, relying on Kitty's more level-headed nature to take care of the minute points. They finished packing their bags and then Mignonne had a moment of clarity, and she and Kitty packed everything except clothes for tomorrow and their toothbrushes, things they could easily shove in their purses, and took their repacked bags and placed them under their beds, hopefully far enough away from the door as not to be readily seen. They needed after all for everything to appear normal tonight. Later that night, after dinner, they'd say that they wanted to go for an after dinner walk outside, and leave their bags somewhere out front, to be grabbed by them before they left for the party tomorrow.

Kitty's nerves felt like they were exploding in her head as she and Mignonne tried to excuse themselves after dinner and go back to their room and grab their belongings, preparing to leave them outside. They weren't running yet, and what they were doing really wasn't against any kind of rules *(besides, who said they had rules in the first place here, dude?)* thought Kitty as she tried to calm her nerves. Kitty decided that there was no reason for her to be nervous in the first place, and sternly told herself to grow up and stop being such a baby about everything. She watched Mignonne pack with envy; Miggy always seemed so confident and self-assured, she sighed out to herself. If she'd been able to really see into Mignonne's head though, her opinion might have changed. Mignonne might have seemed to not have a care in the world, but she was pretty frightened too about the whole thing, operating without allowing herself to stop and dwell on just what it was that she was doing and what she thought the consequences of her current actions might bring. She was just not allowing herself to stop out of fear. She'd learned at a young age that she'd regret something more if she stopped doing it out of nerves than if she did something and it didn't work out, so she had learned to always take her chances with action. She and Kitty finished packing up, and prepared to go to dinner, readying themselves for the action that would commence afterwards.

Everybody tonight seemed so eager to talk and discuss all of the details concerning the party tomorrow with Kitty and Mignonne, and they were kept so busy that they weren't able to escape for a walk outside. So instead of this plan, Mignonne pulled herself away, claiming the need to go the bathroom, and met Kitty's eyes, hoping to convey that she was going to try and get both parcels out of the building and hidden before she was missed. Kitty very pointedly asked Ishept and Indrineela a long and convoluted question about the dogma of this order, making a point to get them just so distracted that they focused on something besides any background action that might be occurring. She was running out of valid questions to ask and was feeling kind of desperate when Mignonne returned, panting a little. Kitty was so relieved to see her back that she let out an involuntary sigh of relief, and

Mignonne tried desperately to catch her breath enough to let her not sound like she'd just finished running a marathon when she was conversing with someone. The night seemed to never end, with more and more people vying for Mignonne's and Kitty's attention, but they finally excused themselves and got back into their room, Kitty seeing with relief that Mignonne had taken her bag outside too, and the two of them tried to calmly brush their teeth and get ready for bed, starting at every little creaking and noise that they heard because their nerves were so keyed up. Eventually they got into their beds and tried to talk about minor issues to calm themselves and not let themselves get bogged down. Now that they initial terror was gone, Mignonne was feeling quite a pleasant rush of adrenaline about their upcoming escape (she couldn't make herself stop thinking of it like it, no matter how little it really might be like a true escape). Eventually she fell asleep out of exhaustion over the excitement of the day, but Kitty laid awake a little longer, looking around the little cave like room that they found themselves in, and thinking that this really wasn't what she had pictured when she first thought of visiting Uncle Clifton overseas.

Chapter 17

The Party

Kitty had a night of fitful sleep where she rolled around a lot and became helplessly entangled in the sheets several times; sheets that felt a lot like burlap now that she was thinking about it. How she wished for the organic total cotton sheets of home! She finally got up later that night, and from her phone clock said that it was about 4:30; Kitty went to the bathroom that she and Mignonne were using and tried to thoroughly brush her teeth, but she felt so keyed up that focus was hard. She finally finished washing off and packed and repacked her bathroom bag; she and Mignonne had decided the night before that to go to breakfast looking any kind of bedraggled might raise suspicion, and neither of them wanted anybody in the either the priesthood or the Elders to suspect anything. Finally, unable to come up with anything else to do, Kitty went and laid back on her bed and tried to be patient as she waited for Mignonne to get up; Kitty reflected that neither storm nor break-in nor nerves of any kind would keep Mignonne from getting a good night's rest. She might not have been so envious of this if she knew the terrifying dreams that always accompanied sleep in these states for Mignonne. Mignonne's phone alarm did wake her up at 6:00, and she got up and saw a slightly drowsing but fully dressed Kitty waiting on her bed. Shaking her head, Mignonne went and got ready herself, though not as quickly as Kitty; attempting to brush her dark dry hair was always an ordeal for her. As she and Kitty left the room and made their way down the corridor to the dining room, she felt her excitement build to a breaking point, and neither she nor Kitty noticed that this was in fact causing some disturbances in the air around her. The air was moving in a circular pattern much faster than normal around her body, responding to the heightened sense of excitement that was generating out of her brain. The girls made their way into the breakfast area, and tried to look like nothing new or exciting was happening today, other than the party of course.

As they were walking towards the breakfast table, Kitty did notice the accelerated air patterns swirling around Mignonne but could not think how to communicate this without notice. She started obsessing over this, terrified that someone else would see and notice, and when they sat down Kitty attempted to make hopefully nonchalant motions with her hand, trying to bring the disrupted air to Mignonne's attention. Mignonne saw this and was not sure exactly what Kitty was trying to communicate at first, but her focusing on what Kitty's motions could mean thankfully took her attention off of their coming escape, and with her attention diverted the air around her did return to normal. It was unfortunate that Ishept was unusually perceptive to details at all times, being a lot like a cabin leader in how she directed people, and she noticed this slight exchange between the girls; her senses immediately went to red alert, and she looked suspiciously at Mignonne and Kitty before demanding to know if they were quite alright. Perhaps a little too hastily, Mignonne and Kitty rushed to assure her that they were, and that they especially were enjoying the breakfast this morning, mm hmm. Ishept let it go after this assurance, but still watched the two with maybe more vigilance than she normally did. Mignonne finally couldn't stand the judgmental gaze anymore and blurted out quite awkwardly that she and Kitty wanted to take a walk. This did nothing to calm Ishept, but she forced herself to smile and say why yes, they were welcome to go for a walk, but perhaps Indrineela might be welcome to accompany them, maybe to tell them a few things about the lovely garden area? Unable to think of a valid reason why Indrineela would not be welcome to come with them, Mignonne and Kitty were accompanied outside and subjected to over an hour of discourse about the unique properties of the garden, starting with an explanation as to how the priestesses managed to keep the willow tree supplied with enough water to enable it to grow in this arid climate. This conversation would have been fascinating to Kitty under any other circumstances, but she was so anxious over the escape plan going awry that both she and Mignonne were only able to hmmm and ahhhh at hopefully appropriate moments, both wishing that Indrineela would suddenly feel the need for a bathroom break or something. After almost two hours of this, Indrineela steered Kitty and Mignonne back into temple, looking quite pleased at the success of her mission to keep the two occupied; whether this was simple good host behavior or she was also suspicious like Ishept, Kitty and Mignonne did not know, but whatever the reason she seemed really high on her success for the morning and their party tonight.

Mignonne and Kitty had no moment alone as they were bustled back into the temple, guided to lunch, and then taken back to a robing room to find clothes appropriate for the evening, with Mignonne getting quite tired of the strict military-like regime, thank you very much. These thoughts were stuffed to the back of her mind however, when she looked with bafflement at their intended attire for the night. The outfits that Ishept had picked out for them looked to be some kind of a cross between a skanky belly dancer and a tacky genie impersonator. Both girls received a midriff top, baggy capri pants, a lot of really audacious jewelry, and strange turban hat looking things; the outfits weren't unlike the bold outfit that they first saw on the priestesses when they came. Kitty's clothes were peach toned and accented with vibrant almost lime green finishing touches, and Mignonne's with sky blue pieces; when the two asked Ishept about this, Ishept assured them that these outfits were designed to showcase their status as the particular Oracles, nothing more. No, Ishept didn't feel that they were under-dressed; this was perfect regalia for the party tonight. Having no choice but to take her word for it, once they had changed completely, Ishept set two priestesses with spending an inordinate amount of time fixing their hair, and Mignonne started to feel more and more agitated as the day wore on, full of people who were constantly around them, and in her mind, watching them closely at all times. She and Kitty were finally deemed dressed and ready for the party, which was ap-parently kind of a big deal, and they were escorted out to a car that was waiting to take them to the soiree.

Not daring to talk in front of the driver should that person possibly speak English, as so many people around here did, the girls sat fidgeting in the back seat, fear building as they approached the house and got farther and farther away from the bags that they had left for their es-cape. Eventually the car pulled up in front of the steps of a huge stone mansion, which seemed to sprawl onwards for miles across the desert, but it was complete with pristine gardens made to look perfect, from the well pruned native trees to the organized flower beds. Breathing deeply, Kitty got out of the car and automatically moved towards the garden areas; the gardens were so very, very immaculate, that Kitty felt sure that the plants and vegetation all were chaffing to grow wild. She felt like she could almost hear them crying, like children who were forced into stiff, formal clothes and not allowed to run and play. So ab-sorbed was Kitty with these thoughts that it took a very loud ahem from Mignonne to remind her that they needed to go inside. The driver was already staring at them in confusion as they loitered on the lawn. Re-luctantly Kitty left the stiff garden and followed her friend up the stairs towards the entrance, which was made up of doors so tall and glassy that she didn't fully understand at first that they were doors at all, and not simply open pathways into the mansion from the outside.

Once Mignonne and Kitty made it past the doorkeeper, showing their tickets that Arkite had given them to the doorman who eyed the two quite suspiciously at first, but as his eyes traveled from their ridiculous genie shoes to their scantily clad upper body, he started to smile lasciviously, his lips curving up. "Oh my goodness, yes ladies. Do please come in. The young masters will be with you shortly," he drawled, and Kitty and Mignonne had been around enough of this to recognize that he might not be verbally making but was definitely thinking about some wildly inappropriate things regarding their purpose at the party. As the two bustled into the entranceway, Mignonne pulled Kitty aside and whispered desperately; "Kitty! I don't think we're dressed like Oracles! I think Ishept dressed us like hookers! I'm not sure what she's hoping will be accomplished with this, or what she expects this night to bring, but I think that we're in trouble! We have to try and get out really quickly!" Quickly nodding her agreement and looking terrified, Kitty grabbed Mignonne's arm and moved back to the huge glass doors to look and see if their ride had left or not; alarm bells were going off in her head ringing crazy loudly, but she tried to think around these thoughts and formulate a plan of escape from this, right now! Before she could think of any reasonable method to get out of this situation, a person came up behind and put his hands on both her and Mignonne's shoulders; they shrieked a little and spun around, but with something like relief that they couldn't explain, they saw Arkite, not an unaccounted stranger assailant. Maybe Arkite did intend to use them in wildly provocative ways but somehow Kitty didn't think so. Meeting his eyes and feeling his hand on her shoulder brought her sudden relief; maybe stupid person relief, but it still helped. Kitty exhaled with relief and even smiled slightly, though Mignonne was apparently not feeling any of this and jerked away from Arkite's hand forcefully, looking at him like either of them might be a rabid animal, breathing rapidly as if preparing for an attack. "Girls. Please calm down. I am only here to talk with the two of you, and…" suddenly a loud crashing of some gongs silenced Arkite's words, and at the other end of the long and wide hallway a raised platform was suddenly occupied with spinning dancing girls; Mignonne noticed that they were not at all dressed unlike her and Kitty, *stupid Ishept*, she thought angrily. They wore reds and yellows, but still the resemblance in the wardrobe was unnerving to Kitty and Mignonne. As they danced like they were attempting to contort their bodies in hitherto impossible ways, a portly older gentleman wearing a turban and formal baggy clothes walked onstage, raising his arms; at his entrance, suddenly the dancing stopped, along with the flickering lights which had been accompanying the movement, and he smiled as if nothing could have pleased him more than to see them all there tonight.

"Old friends! New friends! It is a night of enchantment and magic is this wondrous desert plane! I want to welcome all of you here tonight, and to tell you of the completion of my joy! This year, young master Sphinx will not be alone, but will be accompanied tonight by his wandering brother, young master Arkite! My joy at having my two boys here with me tonight for my annual celebration is unsurpassed, and it is with greatest favor that I wish to relay my blessings on tonight! Please, my honored guests, eat, drink, and make merry amongst yourselves!" At the end of this audacious speech, all of which had been issued at top volume, the fat and jolly master of the house left the podium to tumultuous applause and began wandering the beautifully tiled floor and speaking with one guest after another, smiling with pure joy and clasping their hands gratefully. He was joined in doing this by the handsome and obviously shameless son that Kitty and Mignonne had seen earlier with Arkite, and the two motioned for Arkite to join them. Looking angry and frustrated, Arkite vigorously shook his head no and motioned for Kitty and Mignonne to follow him through a closed door off the hallway, which it turned out also led into a ballroom, though this one was dimly lit and didn't have the decorative splendor of the other ballroom/entranceway. Turning to the two, Arkite gazed at them with hungry eyes; not hungry for anything sexual, but hungrily searching for answers. He looked at Kitty wonderingly as if she were the answer to all of his questions, but Mignonne got tired of this strange look of recognition between the two. She snapped her fingers in front of Arkite's face, trying to bring them both back to the present situation and location, and stop this crazy moon eyed fascination that Arkite seemed to be having for Kitty. Arkite immediately seemed to realize what he was doing, and groggily shook his head as if to clear all of the cobwebs out of his brain and motioned for them to sit on a dilapidated chaise lounge located in one corner of the unused ballroom, while he took a seat in a rickety chair nearby and sat with his eyes closed and head down, massaging his temples as if to make his brain tell him how to begin.

Eventually Arkite's nerves over beginning the conversation were overcome by the driving desire that he felt to speak with Kitty and Mignonne, and eventually he raised his head slowly and then gradually opened his eyes, beginning with quiet words. "I must ask what the two of you are; the Elders and other heretical sects have been trying to recruit me for eons, but with the help of my younger brother I have successfully fended them off." Arkite smiled quirkily as he made this statement, apparently pulling forth some memory that he found still amusing. "I must say that I was not expecting to see the two of you here in Egypt; I know that the Elders are searching rather frantically for the five oracles, but I had no idea that they had been so successful as to get the two of you in their keeping and then out here." Arkite sat back and looked out over the room with an angry expression. Mignonne guessed that he was definitely harboring some kind of spite over their intrusion into his life, but his statement like she and Kitty were allowing themselves to be used by the Elders also irked her. "I have always been unusual in my family, especially when compared to my flamboyant brother. Well, half-brother." Catching the girls questioning eyes he launched into a speech that he'd told so many times to various people that it was beginning to be a bit wearing for him to repeat: "Sphinx and I share a father, but not a mother. I was born from my father's indiscretion with a traveling nomadic woman. His parents did not favor any alliance with this group and forbade him from being with her, although quite obviously this did not work out very well and I came to be. She apparently was quite ashamed of me; perhaps her family also was berating her misbehavior, or maybe she just had no desire to be a mother. Anyway, while the traveling group of nomads was preparing one day shortly after I was born to leave, she appeared at the doorstep here weeping and pleading with him to take me in. She said that she could not keep me any longer for my own safety, and she pressed me into my father's arms and ran off weeping before he could ask any questions. Father did decide to keep me, in spite of my grandparents' consternation. I'm sure you noticed," here again Arkite smiled, "that my father has little care for what everybody thinks, and he withstood the gossip and twittering that accompanied his actions well. He wasn't about to let what the neighbors might say keep him from his first son. At any rate, we continued on against this judgmental tide for a year, but everyone suddenly became preoccupied when his parents made a match that was acceptable and approved by them for him, and they married him off to the daughter of a visiting al-nakhbah. I was around three when my brother was born to them, but alas, my stepmother, whose name was Asima, died in childbirth with him and my father was left with two motherless boys to care for. Shortly after, my grandparents passed away in a tragic automobile accident, and father translated his grief over losing all of his loved ones into how involved he was in our lives, and as the new master of this house he refused to live under anybody else's standards again, and he wouldn't remarry. I tell you these things so that you may understand just how difficult it was for all of us when the Elders came to us when I was thirteen, spinning some story that sounded straight out of 'Arabian Nights.' We had always known that I was different, able to manipulate the people in a room that I was in and hang a shroud of my emotions over everyone there, but I refused to believe them when they said that this was because I was an Oracle. My brother helped me to keep them at bay, and I don't think they dared come see me again after we set the dogs on them the last time that the priestesses came here. Once I saw the two of you and I felt the strange energy coming off of you, I knew that I could no longer ignore whatever was happening in my nature, but that I would have to talk to you." Arkite trailed off here, and looked beseechingly at Kitty and Mignonne, as if he was begging them to believe his words and accept him, freak and bastard child though he obviously thought that he was.

While Mignonne and Kitty sat dumbfounded and staring at Arkite, Mignonne seemed to be struggling with her own internal battles about speaking, trying to find the right words, but she finally looked at Kitty, and then Arkite, before she sat back and breathed. "Huh. So, I guess that's why they brought us out here. To convince you to join them? Well, you'll be relieved to find that we're not going to do that." Mignonne bore a look a determination as she said, "I assume that you bear the Elders no affection, so just know that we are leaving here and leaving their watchful eyes. I'm sick of being used like somebody else's puppet, whatever may be going on with me, and me and Kitty are leaving." Mignonne rose from her seat and looked down at Kitty, wearing her know-it-all smart-aleck look, wearing an expression that Kitty was familiar with, that implied somehow, whether she meant for it to or not, that Kitty would be an idiot if she didn't get up and follow her. Mignonne had actually struggled with having this look and being a much too domineering personality, especially with her friend. It probably came from being the oldest child and having to continually look after Sasha and Caleb, but her mind somehow her started to subconsciously think of Kitty as a younger sister as well, despite the fact that she was only about five months older. Whatever the reason that she had it, even Kitty's sweet disposition had eventually grown tired of this, and occasionally she was forced to reign in Mignonne's parade, so to speak. Mignonne's irritating behavior, coupled with her confusion over the strange feelings that she felt for Arkite, put Kitty over the breaking point.

Kitty did stand up, not to follow Mignonne out, but rather in anger and frustration. It was with this anger and frustration that Kitty looked Mignonne squarely in the eye, and using a tone of voice neither Mignonne ,or anybody, rarely heard, spoke sharply as she said, "Look Mignonne. I'm not about to tell you that this is not a completely weird and possibly dangerous situation, but you know that you're not in charge of the two of us. I have a right to say and do whatever I want, and if I want to leave, I'll leave, but not before. What we, especially I, need to do is sit down and speak with Arkite more about this whole thing, and then decide what to do next. Rushing out of here without any kind of plan isn't a good idea, and it's especially not since we're in a foreign country without any means to pay for transport out of here. We don't even have our luggage. So, I suggest we both sit down, chill out, and then decide what to do." To punctuate her remark, Kitty plopped down on the loveseat abruptly, and stared stonily ahead, not letting herself make eye contact with either Mignonne or Arkite, but quite enjoying her rebellion. Mignonne looked rather dumbfounded, as she always did when confronted with one of Kitty's meltdowns; they happened so rarely that they always surprised her and had more influence on her than more or harsher words from another person would have. Looking chastised, Mignonne sank onto her seat, and both ladies turned back to a silent Arkite, whose silence became even more deafening in the aftermath of this confrontation.

Arkite appeared to be going over in his head exactly how he could best approach this situation, now that he'd seen their dynamic and learned that Kitty was not at all a pushover, as he'd first thought. Mignonne once again found herself exasperated with the quiet that filled the room, though she was still a little cowed by Kitty's shake down, and it was with a softer and more calm voice that she looked at Arkite, forming her words with care: "Okay Arkite. So, we get it. You're an oopsy baby looking for your own place in this world apart from your party animal father and brother. You've seen indications that you might be gifted as an Oracle, but you've always suppressed this to make your family happy. So, that summary leads to the question: what do you want to do now? Because I'll tell you, Kitty and I were planning on running tonight, and if you need our help finding yourself, you'll have to hunt us down." Mignonne was suddenly a little sorry that she'd told him of their plans to leave, but what did it really matter anyway? It's not like he was a good friend of the Elders who'd tell on them anyway, as far as she could see it. Mignonne looked at Kitty as she finished this proclamation, behaving apologetically and inviting Kitty to correct or add to this statement. When Kitty didn't say anything, Arkite decided to answer Mignonne's questions, though he was a little annoyed at her assessment of him as a downtrodden people pleaser. Arkite breathed out and met Mignonne's stare, too nervous to meet Kitty's for some reason. "Well, Mignonne, it does not surprise me that you and Kitty were thinking of leaving the Elders and the Priestesses of the Moon, but perhaps I might be of assistance with this? You see, I have the means to get out and pay for anything that I want; father has always kept me and Sphinx supplied with ample credit cards, though I rarely use mine. We have homes in various parts of the world, and I don't believe that we would be pursued should we go to one. Father has always kept a very secure hold on them. Maybe we could go to one? I cannot escape the binding feeling that I have, that something about me would break if I was separated from you two. I feel with you too that I'm more of myself than I was before; like we're pieces of a puzzle that was designed to go together. So, if you'll allow me to accompany you, we absolutely can leave tonight, and you can have my assistance." As he said this, a look of crazy glee entered his face, as if he was finding wholeness with them and was loathe to think of losing it. He had never before acted impulsively like this, but on the whole it seemed to be a help to him, to make what might have been his first big, solo act.

Kitty and Mignonne both sat looking at Arkite with incredulous eyes, but before they could say anything a loud "Aha!" snapped them out of the moment, and Sphinx bounded into the room. "So, this is

where my dear brother has been hidden away with our lovely guests!"
With blazing eyes and a forced smile, Sphinx seethed as he looked at
Arkite, hissing out, "You dog, you, Arkite. Wandering away from the
party with not one but both of the ladies! I wouldn't have believed it
if I wasn't seeing it myself!" Sphinx let out a nervous laugh as he said
this, looking at Arkite as if begging him to give a different explanation.
Arkite alone with two American girls? This didn't say international
intrigue at all full of suspicious behavior at all... but Sphinx did receive
a different explanation from Arkite, though perhaps not the one he
was hoping for. Arkite stood and faced off with his younger brother,
who though three years younger was much taller and more broad
chested than Arkite. "Sphinx. You are my brother and I love you, but
I am tired of being used as you and father's relative that they wish was
different. I have been feeling more strongly than usual vibrations and
seeing manifestations of what you and father see as a hampering bur-
den much more strongly in myself lately, and I now have an opportunity to go with similar people and maybe find out what this means. I
am leaving, Sphinx. Maybe we can talk again at some point, but right
now I need to do this for *me*. I need to leave." Seeing Sphinx's anger
building and him looking at the girls as if this were their fault, Kitty
surprised Mignonne again for the night and *she* was the one who confronted Sphinx, standing directly in front of him but leaving her hands
open. "This isn't our fault, Sphinx. We said nothing to Arkite about
him leaving, and while we won't get involved in family matters,
neither will we oppose what the other person wants. Everybody
should have the freedom to go and do what they want, no matter what
their family feels like. But we're leaving now, and you two can work
this out on your own time. Kitty looked at Mignonne, who seemed
to read the message she was sending, and stood up with her. Both girls
walked out of the room, down the hallway, and through the doorway,
feeling frazzled and disconcerted.

Chapter 18
Flying Away

Mignonne pulled Kitty off the main driveway and in a section of the yard that was shielded by bushes, though it still consisted mostly of sand, sadly enough. She contritely met Kitty's look, and said much more calmly than she had before, "So. What are we going to do? We have a credit card, and if we can make it to the airport, we could get a flight somewhere. But where?" The very thought of trying to buy and get on an international flight without any idea where they were going mystified Mignonne, and she almost started crying out of confusion and finding herself unable to come up with a valid direction. Should they go home? Somehow, the very thought of this made her want to cry more; there was something happening that she felt couldn't be turned back on, and if she went home, she wouldn't be the same person. A yearning was growing in her, a yearning to learn more about whatever it was that she had or could do, and she didn't think that crawling back home would silence these voices which were starting to clamor in her heart and mind. Mignonne didn't know what to do, so she went back to a fail-safe method that she'd learned a long time ago and go with the decision that gave her peace and that hopefully didn't make her squeamish to think about. As she was trying to find this decision, Kitty grabbed her arm and pulled her farther into the brush. "Come on, Miggy, let's go get our stuff at least." Grateful to at least have a temporary direction, both girls searched in vain for the car and driver that had brought them, forgetting that they'd been intending to run before it returned and that it probably wouldn't be back for another few hours. Mignonne swore softly under her breath; it turned out that they hadn't thought about getting *back* to get their bags if they were left behind before they left on their crazy convoluted adventure, and she was pretty pissed at herself for missing such a minor detail. But at any rate, she and Kitty were dressed like harem girls and they didn't have anything except their purses, which they had carried into the party with them, clutching them for dear life. She tried to remind herself that they weren't quite stranded; they did have a phone, at least. Mignonne and Kitty both pulled their phones out and tried to get them to work, but out here in the middle of who knows where neither of them had reception or much battery life left. This place really drained their phones, which had been charging all of the previous night but now were at 25% battery power, give or take. As both Mignonne and Kitty were looking at their phones and through their purses, Arkite suddenly appeared outside and inched closer to them, seeming to find them with the instinct of a hunter who was listening to the very heartbeats of its prey.

As Arkite moved quickly and agilely through the bushes, much more gracefully than the either of the girls had, before he quite saw them Mignonne whapped him on the face with her purse and she and Kitty went tearing through the foliage, running along the walls of the vast house. "Wait! Please!" Arkite yelled behind them, but neither Kitty nor Mignonne paid any heed to him as they continued their desperate scramble through the plants, unable to really make out where they were going. Hearing a noise and feeling her insides alerting her to danger though, Kitty suddenly stopped and pulled Mignonne also to a stop. For a moment they simply stood there, Kitty trying to find the source of her worry, much less concerned about Arkite's imminent approach than this feeling she suddenly had. Her synapses were still firing, and all of a sudden, she saw the reason why. A considerably large snake slithered out of a pile of wood directly on the path that they were taking, blending in almost completely with the cream colored sand in the moonlight. The snake looked at them, seemed to decide that they were a threat, and advanced menacingly towards them. They stood paralyzed with fear while a slightly panting Arkite came running up behind and stopped. "Do not move. That is a Saharan horned viper, and it will attack if provoked," Arkite breathed behind them, and just as he said this the snake lunged at Kitty, whose previous bravado seemed to have vanished. The air around them seemed suddenly to vibrate and a large gust caught the snake as it was leaping slightly, throwing it and the sand under it a few feet away. Mignonne suddenly felt control of the situation flow into her, and so confident in this, with her using her mind to then force the snake to retreat, keeping it at bay with a strong and constant stream of air, that seemed to grow in size and strength as she focused on it. In a matter of seconds, the snake had disappeared, and an exhausted Mignonne fell tremblingly to her knees, shaking with effort and fear, to be shortly pulled to her feet by Kitty and Arkite, who both looked really stunned.

Arkite and Kitty helped Mignonne to a bench, where she sat shaking, feeling much like recently she'd been falling off a cliff, and was still very possibly falling. Arkite stared at her wide eyed, finally softly saying only, "Wow. So, there may be more to this than I or Sphinx had thought." Looking sheepishly at the two, Arkite held out his hands as if asking without words for forgiveness, though for what they were not sure. "Kitty. Mignonne. Would you two allow me to drive you wherever it is that you're headed? Perhaps we could talk a little more about everything that we are and what should be done?" Grateful to at least not have to walk anywhere as she was still feeling pretty disoriented, Mignonne nodded quickly and Kitty helped her up. They walked with Arkite back to the front of the house, not really caring what happened at this point, and he called somebody on an outdoor intercom speaking brusquely in Arabic and they stood back to wait, staring somewhat awkwardly at each other. A car pulled up to the doorway, and Arkite gently motioned that the girls should get in. But as he himself was getting in, Sphinx again came running out down the stairs leading up to the door, yelling, "Arkite! Please don't do this! If something were to happen to you what would I and father do!?" He seemed genuinely distressed, and as Arkite turned to look at him his gaze softened. "You both would carry on living your lives much as you've always done, I presume, except without me to hold either of you back." "Is that what you think we feel, brother!?" Sphinx blurted, looking both angry at the suggestion and disbelieving that Arkite felt this way. "All of our lives, I have been your brother, and I cannot stand by and watch you go into the unknown by yourself!" Arkite smiled sadly at Sphinx as Sphinx finished saying this and stepped forward and embraced his little brother. "Oh, Sphinx. You must believe, as I do, that I will be fine. I am going to our London house, I believe, and I will contact you when I have arrived." At this Arkite determinedly got back into the back of the car, closing the door very decisively. He said something to the driver, and all three watched as Sphinx faded into the distance, looking shocked and disbelieving.

An awkward silence settled on the car. Well, it was a little awkward for Kitty. While Arkite sat staring determinedly out of the window, though at this time of night there really wasn't anything to see (too dark), Mignonne sat back in her seat and closed her eyes, trying to rub the soreness out of her temples with repeated massaging, unable to believe all that had transpired not just today, but other the past few months. Arkite tapped on window at the driver, and the car, who much to Mignonne and Kitty's alarm, pulled into the driveway of the temple where they had been staying. Both girls looked at Arkite with disbelief; was he seriously taking them back to the one place they were trying to escape!? But before either Kitty or Mignonne could speak, Arkite turned and looked at both girls. Seeing their incredulous look he quickly held up his hands and said, "We're stopping here so that the two of you can grab your belongings. I do expect that the two of you would be amenable to that idea?" Arkite smiled bashfully, looking as though he really had no idea how to work with females, but that he was trying to be considerate. Mignonne thought suddenly that the carefully placed suitcases hadn't come with her and Kitty to the party, but been left out in front of the temple, where they would still be, granted they had not been discovered by the priestesses that is. She felt super annoyed at herself that they had walked out and not thought at all how they would get these when they ran, except maybe if they came back to the temple and grabbed them from a taxi cab or something. Kitty also looked relieved and surprised when the car stopped at the edge of the driveway. She had been so distracted by escaping that she hadn't thought of this either. Arkite motioned for the two to get out once the car had stopped, saying, "I trust you will both want to go and get your belongings inside?" When Kitty and Mignonne rapidly explained what they'd done, Arkite actually sat back and laughed, a most pleasing sound since he was usually so serious. "So, you two always intended to run? Even before you talked to me and came to our family party? How classic!" "Yes well, it was part of a poorly planned escape route that we had but hang on and we'll get the stuff" Mignonne said pertly as she and Kitty got out of the car and walked a little up the path. She was feeling a little embarrassed as she opened the car door and dug through the shrubbery and extracted hers and Kitty's luggage.

The air was cooler than it had been earlier tonight, quite pleasant in fact, and a soft breeze was blowing as Kitty and Mignonne went into the bushes and retrieved the bags from where Mignonne had left them. Feeling relieved that they were almost home-free, so to speak, as they were walking back to the car a voice behind them coming from the temple startled them. "What are you doing, Oracles!? You're not running away are you? The Elders will be most displeased!" Mignonne and Kitty turned to see Indrineela running after them, having been alerted to their presence by car sensors at the beginning of the driveway possibly; or maybe she had seen them get out and get their bags. That was as far as Mignonne's thoughts could go, anyway. When Indrineela caught up to them, her expression was both worried and angry. Apparently the Elders were kind of a big deal with her order; or maybe she was just pissed that their hospitality would be treated like this. Before Mignonne could think of what to say, it was Kitty was jumped in. "Yes, Indrineela. We don't much like how you guys and the Elders are using us, so we're going to leave before we become even more of a tool. So, goodbye!" At this Kitty turned to march back to the waiting car, where Arkite had gotten out to check if the situation was in control. And sweet Indrineela looked at them with venom in her eyes, and she began muttering something that seemed to be causing disturbance and warping reality around them. They suddenly felt that they had no firm hold on the ground and that it was slipping out from under them, while the rest of what they saw, the building, the yard, the car, starting swirling in complex geometric patterns, looking absolutely fluid and moving upside down, much as they did for Alice in Wonderland. As Mignonne and Kitty were shrieking and trying to gain a foothold is the rapidly moving world, more priestesses started coming towards them. Arkite realized what was happening to them and raised his hands into a "Stop" motion; quite suddenly everything in the world started to slide back into place, and Kitty and Mignonne scrambled to their feet. Arkite didn't even look at them but rasped out, "Quickly. Get in the car. I'm not sure how long I can keep her illusion at bay!" In fact, the world seemed to be distorting again as the girls opened the car doors and fell into the seats. Arkite was shaking and dripping with sweat as he dropped in after them, telling the driver something quickly as the car started to move. The driver looked alarmed as the world kept moving inside out and he hit the brakes in terror, screeching. Arkite tried to pull himself together as he rasped something at him, speaking unceasingly in Arabic. Eventually the driver started to tentatively move the car again, in spite of the warping reality, and thankfully this distortion only lasted about another 600 feet. As they continued down the road, Mignonne looked at Arkite with astounded eyes, eventually managing to whisper, "What did you do? What did *they* do?" Looking pretty astonished himself, Arkite put his hands on his face and shook his head as he clarified, "I noticed that the priestess was warping reality, but before I could panic, I realized that it was not real. It was only an illusion that she was using, confusing your eyes and senses into thinking that she was manipulating reality and that you were being thrown around. The Elders, and some of the priestesses, can distort things like that; but it is not real," he added decisively. "They are not able to really change reality in any kind of way, just trick the eyes into thinking it is so. My supposition is that one of the reasons that they are so desperate to obtain the cooperation of the Oracles because the Oracles can work with true matter, not just appear to do so."

Head spinning even more than her body previously had been, Mignonne looked at Arkite and with a very confused voice blurted out, "So, then it's all true? The Oracles are a real thing, and not just something to get us to listen to them?" Arkite smiled and nodded, looking at Kitty and Mignonne with something like relief. "It would appear to be so. I have long studied this idea of the Oracles, in fact since I was first approached with the idea that *I* was one. They told me that I was the Oracle of the element *Ether*, which I had no idea what that was then. It turns out ether is something that long ago scholars saw as existing in all reality, forming matter alongside the atoms and cells. This supposition was eventually debunked, but I was told that I have the ability to manipulate this supposedly non-existent property; that I could order and augment reality into forming what I chose, and it seems now that I can also return reality to its natural state!" At this pronouncement Arkite actually threw his head back and laughed, looking joyous and relieved that he wasn't in fact crazy. "I thought that the priestesses were making up stories to confirm my family's cooperation, both monetarily and with their dealings with the government. After all, my father is something of a sheik. I wasn't aware that that is truly what I was doing all this time, though! Oh ladies, we can do marvelous things!"

Kitty and Mignonne started chirping excitedly with Arkite, about what they were and what they could possibly do with this, and before long the driver pulled the car up to the airport, where they all tumbled out, still riding a strange high from the discoveries of the night. So giddy were they, in fact, that at first they did not notice the solemn looking figure who was waiting outside the terminal. They weren't sure exactly how he'd gotten there ahead of them, but they suddenly heard, "Sphinx!" shouted an astonished Arkite. "What are you doing here?" Suddenly thinking of a possible reason, Arkite's countenance immediately clouded, and with steely eyes he barked out, "You cannot stop us. We're leaving, on the next flight to England if possible. There's nothing that you, nor father, can do." Sphinx looked astonished at this remark and stepped backwards; "Whoa, whoa, whoa, Arkite, slow your roll! I'm not here to stop you! I just wanted to say goodbye and say that I would at least like you to contact me when you get settled," Sphinx shrugged at this, and Arkite looked immensely relieved. He obviously didn't want conflict with his brother, but after a while, his relief gave way to suspicion. "Alright Sphinx, so you will not mind if we all proceed into the building?" Arkite spoke, almost daring Sphinx to oppose him. But now that he saw that his brother was really thinking of going, Sphinx shook his head no and stepped aside, letting an anxious Mignonne and Arkite go through the doors by themselves and then eagerly stepping forward and holding the door for Kitty. Sphinx flashed Kitty a brazen smile as he did so, and finished off with a wink, still sounding amused as he called after his brother, "Arkite! Try your best to actually interact with more people, okay?" before he allowed the door to swing shut behind them. Kitty and Mignonne turned upon entering and looked into the daunting airport terminal.

Though the two had arrived there earlier, they were still flabbergasted by the sheer amount of things that was going on around them.

Billboards, signs, posters, all with unintelligible writing on them, and a mass of people milling about and hurrying from terminal to terminal. Some women wore varying degrees of the typical Muslim hi 'jab, dressed covered and modest, but not all women did this. Some men scurried back and forth on their cell phones, carrying briefcases and wearing formal attire, both Western and traditional. But in all this it was the simple enormity of the amount of people that first took Mignonne's and Kitty's breath away. Not that they hadn't been in the airport before, but that it would still be so crowded as the day turned into night, still so alive with the coming and goings of different branches of humanity astounded them. It was a good thing that Arkite at least seemed able to decipher the seeming gibberish on the signs, and he marched up to a counter where he started talking to an attendant, motioning back at Kitty and Mignonne and all the bags. The clerk saw what the girls were wearing and gave Arkite a knowing smile, cutting his eyes at them as he went on talking with Arkite presumably about the tickets. Mignonne was getting really fed up at being treated like an a high end prostitute who was accompanying her employer, and she sighed and clucked her tongue, grabbing Kitty's hand and their bags and walking towards the bathroom. On their way off Kitty stopped and pointed for Arkite where they were going, and once inside the stalls both girls pulled off their ridiculous and scandalous clothing and put on dresses and slacks that were less revealing. Deciding to leave the hooker clothes in the bathroom, Mignonne and Kitty made their way once again to the counter where Arkite was now waiting. "I have purchased tickets for us, ladies," Arkite murmured, "But unfortunately the flight does not leave for another two hours. Let's go sit down somewhere and try to stay inconspicuous, we don't know who the Elders are now going to send after us." Nodding their assent, Kitty and Mignonne followed Arkite farther into the airport and into the boarding terminal designated for the London flight that was leaving next, and they all sat waited for their flight, nervously looking over their shoulders as

169

if the priestesses, or the Elders, or anybody really, might suddenly appear in their line of sight and cause a ruckus even in the airport.

The two hours passed agonizingly slowly as the three were so keyed up, but pass they did eventually, and using Arkite's direction when something that sounded like a boarding call was came over the intercom, Mignonne and Kitty followed the thronging crowd through the ticket counter and up into the waiting plane. Finding their seats was no problem (like they had when arriving at the priestesses' temple, they again matched the symbols on their tickets to the markings over the seats to verify their places), and all three settled in for the seven-hour flight, all of them looking around in a very bewildered fashion, as if not quite able to comprehend everything that had happened and how they felt, not really believing yet that they had gotten away. Kitty felt nothing but relief as the flight took off, as if she'd been dreading that somehow someone would stop their flight and take them back. Mignonne was still going over and over in her mind what happened when she was defending Kitty earlier, wondering what it meant and if that kind of power was something that she could learn to control. She thought of Arkite's bizarre affiliation with ether, whatever that was, Taylor's manipulation of water, and her own command of the air surrounding them and wondered what it all meant. Kitty hadn't yet experienced anything to convince her of her powers as an Oracle, but she did think of the other's gifts as real and powerful, while she wondered desperately if she had anything like that. Kitty didn't know, but she had a tingling and trembling feeling watching the others that she thought showed a possible connection. At any rate, Mignonne soon grew tired of these ponderings, and leaned her head back to try and doze through the fortunately peaceful air currents.

Kitty and Mignonne were both jolted out of their light sleep when they were suddenly lifted upwards in their seats; the plane seemed to stop in midair and it began shaking, with the windows showing them shifting clouds and an off-balance plane. They could see the windows almost seeming to separate from the plastic paneling as if the whole plane was coming apart, but that wasn't possible, was it!? Mignonne frantically looked across the aisle at Arkite, who appeared to be undergoing some sort of a rapid analysis of the situation in his head, sitting with his hands tensed on the arm rests of his seat, leaning forward with a harried look on his face, his eyes darting around wildly and breathing quickly. It was what a runner would sound like after they completed 10k that they had never stopped or slowed down during, and Mignonne worried that he was about to completely lose it. The only other time she'd seemed someone be as frantic as this was when her schizophrenic great uncle, at a family reunion, had a negative reaction to a new medication and began hyperventilating at some unknown trigger that nobody in her family ever discovered. He was rushed to the nearest hospital by his son, her real uncle, and her Dad spent most of the rest of that day on the phone with his brother or any other family member, trying to remain up to date on what was happening and trying to remain above the anxiety so that he could assist if needed. She'd been young when this happened, but the frantic look on Arkite's face reminded her of the way that her great uncle's face looked right before he completely lost it, and like then, she found herself frightened and not knowing what to do. Not knowing what else to do, Kitty got up and though the plane was now pitching violently, stumbled over to the vacant seat next to Arkite. Feeling oddly calm amidst all the chaos and yelling, Kitty placed her hand on Arkite's shoulder and she met and held his gaze. Suddenly someone starting announcing over the speaker system in what sounded like a muddled version of Arabic, and having been returned from the brink of hysteria, Arkite turned to Kitty, and then Mignonne, and with panic in his eyes told them that due to some unforeseen atmospheric turbulence the plane would be making an emergency landing in Alexandria, according to the pilot.

As the three buckled their seatbelts against the rapid descent of the airplane onto a landing strip in the nearest airport in Alexandria after about five minutes of shaking, with stewards trying desperately to keep everyone in their seats and to keep them calm, and dropped abruptly onto the tarmac, skidding to a stop to compensate for the much-shorted landing that the pilot had been forced to drop down on. As Kitty and Mignonne were pushed and hurried along by the other passengers, who all seemed to be trying to make the quickest departure from the plane as humanly possible, they lost sight of Arkite for a brief time and began visually searching for him with much anxiety. Mignonne pulled Kitty off to the side once they were inside the new terminal and tried to fight rising panic by not allowing herself to think that she was a young woman, alone without any practical self-defense training, in the middle of a foreign airport with no way to contact anyone who could possibly help her. She was about to really lose it when her head turned frantically and she spotted Arkite; both his arms were being held to his side by two men that she did not recognize and he was being frog-marched towards her and Kitty. "Well, well, well," came a melodious and familiar voice behind them. "You three really have given us quite the how-do-you-say, *run for our money?* Tut, tut ladies, this really was unnecessary, considering that really, all the Elders and the priestesses wanted to do was train the Oracles how to use your powers. Perhaps you could help us once you learned them, hmmm?" Omage smiled sadistically as he finished this statement and told his compatriots in what sounded like French something. He motioned them towards some seats nearby, where they quite unceremoniously pushed Arkite down, maintaining a military hold on his arms at all times. "Mignonne, Kitty. You two and Arkite will spend the rest of tonight in here in Alexandria under constant guard, and come morning you will be flown to London, where the Elders will discuss amongst ourselves how best to keep you contained. I trust that you will give us no trouble in this endeavor, hmmm?" Omage once again smiled psychotically as he said this, obliviously not anticipating any trouble from them, but his barely concealed anger and frustration made Mignonne really want to fight back. At the very least, she thought desperately to herself, she could incapacitate his knee caps and then she and Kitty could run? She could name a problem with this idea right from the get go; for starters, would she be able to break his knees before either him or his bodyguards could react and grab her? Also, what if Kitty, who was usually so attune to her mind, chose this one moment to not be paying attention in this panic? She finally thought about Arkite; would this mean that they would leave him to the mercy of his captors, and what would *that* mean? They'd just met the guy for goodness' sake, but could she reconcile her mind to leaving another hostage behind. Before she could finish this thought, Omage put his hand up and muttered something; the air around them suddenly seemed very warm, and their minds very drowsy and incoherent. The last image that Kitty had before her eyes rolled back in her head and she passed out, not unlike her rapid response to really good hospital anesthesia, was of Arkite struggling madly and shrieking, while the airport walls seemed to be receding in and out and his guards stumbled over the no shifting ground, releasing him. Right after this Kitty passed out, and an extremely perturbed Omage fought to maintain his balance while he approached the now free Arkite, back- handing him across the head with considerable force and yelling at his comrades to get the hell up and bring the three now prostrate bodies outside, muttering about how this had been too damn close, and the Elders would accept no more troubles with the plans.

Chapter 19

Fighting Away

Kitty suddenly woke up in a dark stone room, laying sprawled out on the floor by herself. She frantically pulled herself up and started looking for Mignonne, groping around the stone walls and along the floor, searching for something, *anything*, to be there. Kitty finally concluded that she was alone in this little box room and she sat back, her heart pounding and her mind darting with running rabbit speed over options about a) where she was, b) where Mignonne was, and c) what she was going to do to get herself out this situation. Her mother had insisted that she take self-defense classes, but not thinking that she'd ever need any of this she hadn't really paid attention. Silently berating herself for this, she wondered what kind of options she would have, although since she had no idea where she was and what was happening, she was really at a disadvantage at being able to plan for anything. As she was thinking these things what she guessed was a regular doorway was swung open, and light flooded in from a hallway. Some other guard, a woman this time, helped a stumbling Mignonne in and sat her down on the floor. The lights came on as she crouched down next to Miggy, listening to her heart with a stethoscope and giving her a quick temperature check and eye exam, muttering about how stupid the other Elders and priestesses were behaving, that this girl was having some kind of adverse reaction to whatever Omage had done to her and could quite easily have died had she, the doctor, not been close. Finally concluding that Mignonne's wasn't about to completely check out on her, the lady-doctor-Elder/priestess stuffed her tools back in her bag and stomped out of the room, slamming the door behind her. So inordinately happy to see her friend was Kitty that she scuttled across the stone floor and hugged Mignonne, who at first seemed really out of it but eventually attempted to put her arms up and return the embrace. "Kitty?" came Mignonne's trembling voice, "What happened? Are you okay?" Assuring Mignonne that she was alright, at least for now, Kitty and Mignonne began rapidly talking through what had happened, where they could possibly be, and where was Arkite? Was he hurt? Dead, even? Neither liked to think about that thought but figured that in desperate times such as these they were forced to face the worst. Both girls were actually starting to get hungry by the next time the door opened again, what seemed like hours later, and two new guards came in and pulled the two of them to their feet, forcing them out the room while silently withstanding a flurry of indignant questions from Kitty and Mignonne as to what the hell was going on and who they were. Not deigning to reply, the guards pushed them out of the room and down a short hallway, shoving them into another room. When Mignonne looked up, she was glad to see Arkite (though he was a bound and gagged Arkite), but she didn't have much time to think before a new individual stood up.

This newcomer did not appear to have any distinctive race or nationality, but to rather be the flotsam combination of African and Caribbean descent. He, because he quite obviously was a man wearing too tight pants, stood and faced the two girls. Now that they stopped to look the girls also saw Omage standing in the background, seemingly cowering in the presence of this man, whose black eyes seemed to hold no patience with the situation any longer. Moving with the demeanor of a man who was accustomed to being obeyed, this person stepped forward and made eye contact with Kitty and Mignonne, and while a pertinent comment had been on Mignonne's lips something in this newcomer's expression kept both her and Kitty silent. His hands extended in front of him, in an aura of perfect mastery of the situation and everyone in the room, he began to slowly and melodiously speak. "Oracles. I am pleased to have you here, though this situation does lead something to be desired, don't you think? You, Arkite, have been especially recalcitrant, and it is only because of your newness with which you have come into this situation that is keeping you from abject punishment." He looked at Arkite loftily, with something closely akin to revulsion, before he continued. Turning back to face Kitty and Mignonne he spoke again, so softly that had they not been paying desperate attention they would have missed it. "I am Sagta, and I am here to clean up the mess that my fellow Elders have made of this situation in Scotland and here in Africa. Omage is very fortunate not only that he was able to bring the three of you so easily to heel because you lack any real training, but also that his actions in Scotland did not before this time come to my attention. I have brought all of you here to Alexandria so that I may clean up this mess and bring the Oracles truly under control." Sagta here narrowed his eyes and without turning reached up and snapped his fingers. A table was rapidly brought in, along with chairs, and a large pot placed in the center, the smell coming off of it reminding Kitty and Mignonne just how hungry they were. Sagta smiled ruefully at the three of them. "Well, in any event you three must eat to retain your stamina so you will be prepared for *true* training in your abilities, starting with a discourse on why the Oracles are fated to work with the Elders in maintaining order in this world." Sagta motioned that the guards guide the girls to chairs and release their arms, though they remained in the room and Arkite's two guards remained directly behind him. "Eat, my friends. You must be famished, after all," Sagta finally said, and he strode out of the room, leaving them with bowls and spoons and a quite decadent smelling stew to partake of.

Before they even thought of eating, Kitty and Mignonne looked at Arkite, as if desperately wishing for him to have any idea of what to do. He smiled sardonically at them, and with a shake of his head indicated that they could not talk in front of these guards, who very well might understand and report on them. He slowly and deliberately picked up his spoon, filled it with lentil soup, and quite obviously brought it to his mouth, never taking his eyes off the guards. Mignonne also took courage from this, and she leaned forward and began whispering madly to Kitty about how they could escape and return stateside. Kitty only seemed to be catching about half of this and contented herself to smiling and nodding like a maniac, hoping to keep attention off Mignonne's words of insubordination. Suddenly, a loud crash and shaking of the ground started, almost to the degree of a minor earthquake, and the guards immediately ran to the door to find out what was happening. They saw something and ran towards it, leaving the three of the Oracles sitting there with the stew. Waiting for no other reprieve, Arkite leapt to his feet and ran to the door, and since they were not much desiring being left behind, Kitty and Mignonne also jumped up and ran after him just in time to hear him issue an exultation in Arabic and dash down the hall. Mignonne and Kitty also ran after him, and as they approached whatever pandemonium was occurring down the hall the saw a mass of Elders of every race imaginable attempting to subdue Taylor (*Taylor?* thought Kitty), and yet another unnamed person. This other person looked to be about their age, and they heard Taylor yell, "Justin! You go left, I'll go right!" The left side of the room was suddenly inordinately hot as flames leapt away from this new person, and while Mignonne's first instinct was to leap away from the flames, Kitty was feeling something deep inside of her thrumming in response to the action, growing stronger and stronger, as if a long-repressed instinct was answering a call. As she lifted her arms, sand starting coming through the cracks and gaps in the stone flooring, accompanied by tamarisk and markh vegetation. She couldn't tell if they were big bushes or small desert trees, but carried by the rush of sand they came at the group of Elders from behind, trapping their legs in the sand and keeping their small magical abilities at bay from an ambush of sand and plant life that took them from behind, and the room was suddenly filled one side from the front of a flood of rushing water and the other an engulfing torrent of flames with an encroaching torrent of plant life threatening them from behind.

Mignonne saw this and was desperate to help, but she also saw that the only area not being covered by elemental madness was above. The Elders seemed also to notice this, and they began scrambling for higher ground away from the flood, the fire, and the avalanche of earth. Not knowing what else to do, Mignonne closed her eyes and began imagining strong winds, like from a tornado or, better yet, a hurricane rushing into the room and carrying the Elders away. Winds as strong as either of these natural disasters did not happen, but she felt her body thrumming as she called forth strong enough air that began rushing into the room through the windows, the windows being shattered already by the sand and plant life. The force of wind came rushing along the halls from the open doors into the room, making it impossible for the Elders to make and retain any type of hold or balance on their surroundings, no matter how high they were grasping, despite the small spells that they were attempting to thrust at the Oracles, much as they had done in the airport to subdue them. These incantations were not proving effective against the tide of madness surrounding them, but before the Oracles could exult too much, Kitty and Mignonne saw as a new player stepped on the field.

The Elders saw this individual too, and cries of strangled joy escaped their lips. Sensing some new power player presence, Mignonne and Kitty turned just in time to feel themselves being lifted off their feet and thrown against a wall, them and everyone else in the room, all four of the Oracles and the Elders, by a very irate Sagta. Sagta took his time approaching them, holding his arms straight down and seeming to enjoy their paralysis. His eyes flicked like an angry, predatory large cat, and what sounded like a cross between a growl and a mass of angry mutterings came from his throat. Kitty and Mignonne both struggled desperately to get up, feeling the same fear as a caged animal must feel when it is unable to move or defend itself. Taylor had been knocked unconscious, and Kitty saw that this new character, Justin, seemed to be barely hanging on to his consciousness as he tried to use the wall to stand up, much without success. As Mignonne's eyes darted wildly side to side and she instinctively tried to back up, encountering only another wall, her breath came rapidly, and she struggled to regain control of her mind. Perhaps this was it, some corner of her consciousness thought? Despair consumed her at this thought, though it came with less fear than she would have anticipated. Instead, some sort of bleak determination took hold and she closed her eyes, not much wanting to see the end as it came. *Could you see death as it approached*, she wondered with a strand of her thinking that wasn't consumed with other things. Kitty, who still had her eyes open, saw Sagta grinning manically and triumphantly, a very pleased expression on his face. Clearly, he was feeling that he hadn't underestimated the Oracles' level of control of their gifts. Victory seemed assured, when something that he hadn't planned on or even thought of happened.

None of the Elders who hadn't been knocked out completely by something or other of the Oracles or Sagta had noticed in the mayhem that they were dealing with only four Oracles. The simple desperate fight for survival that they had been engaged in had been sufficient in keeping them totally occupied with the four in the room, and even the four Oracles present hadn't had time to stop and think about the fact that someone was missing. Maybe it was because so much had been changing and happening in their lives that certain details went missing. Maybe it was because they hadn't truly developed any real rapport with the other three Oracles, with the possible exception of Taylor. At any rate, in the middle of her horror it suddenly occurred to Kitty that someone was indeed missing. Almost simultaneously to this thought, all of the air around her seemed to fall still, with people's mouths opening in screams that did not produce a sound. Sagta's own eyes widened in panic as the realization dawned on him of what was happening, but as he slowly opened his mouth, to scream or utter other incantation, nobody knew, he was suddenly thrust down forcefully on his knees, a position that he wasn't able to get up from. In fact, all of the Elders were unable to stand, and many of them were trying to scream in pain as they clutched their legs and knees. Arkite, the figure that neither of the girls had noticed was missing, was now making his way into the room.

Arkite was shaking as he made his way to the center, finally collapsing under his weight on his own buckling knees once he reached it, with his eyes closed and panting. He felt his own control of the ether that permeates the universe fighting against his control, and sensing his own death, he hoped that this had been enough. Seeing Arkite and watching his room crushing power display made Mignonne and Kitty both want to yell in triumph, but as they watched him fall, a still, small voice spoke to them and said that Arkite needed help. He couldn't hold onto this control much longer. Not knowing or caring where this voice came from, Kitty and Mignonne each scrambled to their feet. Thankfully, the matter in their own bodies wasn't being affected by Arkite's control of ether, Kitty guessed because he was somehow being selective with his control of it, and they exchanged one look before they ran towards Arkite, shrieking in joy and suddenly feeling full and completely in control of their own elements. Without using any effort that she could feel, Kitty commanded, rather than timidly asking, the surrounding earth and vegetation that she had started to bring into the room earlier in the conflict to continue to grow and bury the Elders. The stone walls and floors in this the abode of the Elders began to crumble and she pulled the sand and the accompanying growth, at break-neck speed, into the chamber, willing it to invade the room and cover the Elders, feeling its unharnessed power in doing so.

While Kitty was very much involved with doing this, Mignonne used the force of her gift of air to lift herself and Kitty out of the way of the landslide of desert paraphernalia, her wind protecting them and rattling the windows and the walls, finally bringing them and the Elders who were not buried crashing down and flinging them apart across the distance of a football field. The tornadic wind crushed the sand on top of the Elders, compacting the earth over them into a firmly sealed tomb from which they couldn't escape; at least, not within any short period of time or without great effort. Her last thought, before she and Kitty passed out from exertion, was that man, she hoped that they managed to pull the other Oracles out of the sand. She didn't want to be responsible for a quick end of the time of the Oracles. This idea was the last thought that she was aware of, before she and Kitty both fell about two feet and hit the sand, crumbling up, with their minds completely checking out into blessed unconsciousness.

Chapter 20

Awakening

Kitty awoke lying on a little couch, with an IV in her left elbow and a slowly diminishing bag of fluids located to her side. As the memory of what had just transpired came rushing back to her, she frantically tried to scramble to her feet, panicking lest the Elders had won after all and she was in their custody, with Mignonne and the others having who knows what done to them. Alas, the second that she placed her feet on the floor and attempted to stand she collapsed onto her knees once again, her legs feeling too weak to hold her up and her heart racing with the effort. Her IV had come crashing down to the ground as she went towards the floor, and the crash apparently alerted someone to her wakefulness. After hearing a few sounds of feet pounding the hallway and the muttering of voices, the door was flung open and Kitty saw a priestess named Amira who Kitty had seen before using her skills as a healer came bursting in. Kitty again freaked out upon seeing her, and once more she tried without success to stand up and get away from this personage. The doctor-priestess Amira seemed to anticipate this, and she slowed her walk into the room, and motioned those who came to help her to stay away.

She sank down onto her knees in front of Kitty, smiling slowly and holding her own hands out in front of her, in an unmistakable surrender postulation. "My distinguished *almushawir alhakim*, neither I nor your gracious hosts intend to harm you. You are in the home of the distinguished master Akhon Silveraii. I believe that you are acquainted with his sons?" "Hell, yeah she knows us! Hi, pretty Kitty, how's it going?" A new voice chimed in audaciously as the doctor finished murmuring this, and the door once again was flung open wide and ignoring the voices in the hallway trying to stop him, Sphinx strode in and smiled rakishly.

Suddenly seeing Kitty, who was still prostrate on the floor, Sphinx stopped walking and immediately rushed to Kitty's side, standing the IV fluid holder back up and then taking her by the arms and returning her to the couch. Swearing slightly, without turning around, Sphinx threatened the doctor with the usual (death, dismemberment, disembowelment), and the healer flung up her hands in exasperation and wisely chose to take her leave from the room at that time. Still shaking with her heart racing, Kitty looked at Sphinx, feeling really grateful to see a familiar face, even one she'd only met twice before. "That bizarre doctor-priestess said that she was switching allegiances, so to speak, and asked to be allowed to care for you guys. But father wasn't stupid enough to let her in without supervision, and she came in here by herself for the first time just now. Did she push you or hurt you?" Sphinx looked at Kitty with mingled hope and despair. Finally recognizing what had happened, Kitty began to laugh nervously and weakly. "No, Sphinx. It's fine. I fell, and she must have heard me fall. She never touched me once I was awake." Relief flooding Sphinx's face, he still looked at the doorway and scowled at the now-absent doctor. "Here," Sphinx said, standing up and extending his hands to Kitty, "You should come with me and see your friend. She is awake and has been asking for you." Sphinx led Kitty down the hall only a little ways, and he stopped and opened the second door on the left from them. "Mignonne!" he trilled,

"Someone is here to see you!" In excitement Kitty lurched forward and fell across the seat where Mignonne was sitting, hugging her while simultaneously both girls started yammering rapidly. Mignonne, who had been awake slightly longer than Kitty, told her what she'd learned: After she and Kitty had managed to bring down the house (she smiled ruefully as she said this), the strain had completely depleted their energy stores and they had passed out. But Arkite and the doctor both said that this was just because they weren't used to using their abilities, especially within that magnitude, and with time and training they would get better at it and could withstand more exertion. After they had fallen out, Arkite had managed to pull himself out of the sand and using his spidey-senses or something had searched out the auras of the other two Oracles Taylor and Justin. Calling his brother for help, they had unearthed the Fire Oracle and the Water Oracle, in that order, when Arkite lost it, and Sphinx kindly brought all of the then unconscious Oracles back to his dad's house, though she wasn't entirely sure how this had been done. Still looking slightly dumbfounded at what she and Kitty had done, Mignonne wearily gave up on talking and explaining everything, saying that they'd just have to wait and talk more with Akhon tonight; he'd been nice enough to invite them to dinner, after all, should they feel up to it.

Following a brief and necessary respite, Mignonne and Kitty changed back into their freshly laundered jeans and shirts, Mignonne swept her hair up with a clip that she found in a side table, because she didn't want to be caught underdressed at dinner, after all (she caught Kitty rolling her eyes in exasperation as she said this). The two were led down the hall to the dining room by a quiet steward, who left them alone once reaching his hand out to indicate the table and the seats. Shortly after they were seated, a much less joyous than usual Akhon strode in, followed by his two sons. "Well, my lovely *almushawir alhakim*, I am most pleased to see the two of you well enough to join us for dinner tonight." A wan looking Taylor and this new guy

Justin were helped in by several more stewards, and Akhon smiled as he saw them. He snapped his fingers and servants who'd been apparently waiting for this sound bustled in, depositing dishes and trays full of food on the table and then departing. "Please, everyone, sons and guests, partake of this abundance," Akhon then opened one of the dishes closet to him and began spooning chicken and rice onto his plate. Mignonne, however, was unable to wait any longer before finding out what life might bring to them next, and sat forward, almost falling out of her chair and forcing Arkite to meet her gaze.

"What now, Arkite?" Mignonne asked desperately. She felt that if she at least at some sort of idea about what might happen next, she would be so much more able to handle it. It was sitting here with no earthly idea that was killing her, and once again she felt her heart rate accelerate as she said this. The other Oracles were grateful for Mignonne's impatience and utter lack of refinement at the dinner table, and they all looked at Arkite and Sphinx. Sighing deeply, as though he had anticipated this question but still held it in dread, Arkite placed his utensils that he'd been holding down, and began speaking. "Mignonne. Kitty. Taylor. Justin. I am in gratitude to the Higher Power that you four are here with me, and that we made it away from the Elders with minimal fuss." "Minimal fuss!? What the hell are you talking about!? Maybe you weren't there the whole time and didn't see, but Taylor and I kicked ass! Mignonne and Kitty had to jump in and help your sorry, pampered butt!" Justin spoke rapidly and panted as he said this. Apparently he was a man who didn't believe in not speaking his mind, regardless of the circumstances. Reaching out his arm to quiet the now irate Sphinx, Arkite shushed his brother, turning to Justin and saying, "No. Justin is quite right. Considering how very little the four of you have known of training or developed your abilities everyone did a remarkable job. So remarkable, in fact, that perhaps we give to give credit to a possible divine intervention?" Arkite smiled sardonically before he continued, "Regardless of whatever it was that transpired, I think that we can all agree that phenomenal things transpired, and it is necessary for all of us to sit together and discuss what comes next."

"When we were accosted by the Elders, Mignonne, Kitty, and I were on our way to the London house that our family owns. We all saw today how barely we survived without either skill development or unification among our minds as to our actions. Therefore, it is my proposal that Kitty, Mignonne, and I continue on this trip, and dwell together so that we may begin to sync our gifts into a usable force to be reckoned with." Arkite smiled somewhat sarcastically again as he faced Justin and Taylor. "Or course, the two of you are welcome to join us for this time of training and comradery. Please though, Justin, try and keep your own disgruntlement and agitation shaped down into a dull roar?" Before a very put out Justin could respond, Kitty, Mignonne, and Taylor started chattering eagerly to Arkite, but Kitty stopped almost immediately and looked at Sphinx. Sphinx was trying to smile happily, but his look held some of the sad clown look, and he looked resigned but still distressed and sad. Standing rapidly, he flung his napkin down on the table and mumbled an excuse as he started to leave the table, feeling left out and disconnected from not only his brother now, but all of these new people as well. Even if Sphinx got on his nerves, he was still Arkite's younger brother, and the older brother mentality was apparently still strong in Arkite as he also stood from the table and said, "Wait, Sphinx! I know all of this is new, and new things are often frightening and baffling, but I don't want you to know, or feel, that I am leaving you behind in any sort of way. After all, Sphinx, it is our father's London house that we are thinking of going to. I would feel quite honored if you should choose to accompany us, although of course I understand if you have your own plans." Arkite bowed with somewhat awkward integrity after he said this, and he glanced furtively at his brother to see how this offer would be received. Sphinx seemed to be wrestling with himself. He still didn't want to feel like his older brother was condescending to him, but his pride was overshadowed when he looked at Kitty.

Sphinx began striding around the table to his brother, who apparently wasn't quite sure that he wasn't being attacked in some way and put up his hands to block any blows that were coming. Sphinx didn't stand on formality as he grabbed Arkite's arm and pulled him into a hug, slapping his back and laughing. "Oh Arkite, you shouldn't have!" Sphinx intoned breezily. "But, dear brother, what on earth would I do with you and the rest of the Oracle brigade, pray tell?" Akhon chose this moment to break in, and it was with a yearning for love between his children that he tentatively made the suggestion, "I am sure, Sphinx, that while Arkite and the other *almushawir alhakim* are working towards perfecting their abilities together, that you would be welcomed as a type of security detail? They'll be distracted of course, and not always able to watch for attack. I am certain that the Elders and the priestesses that the ladies were with, and perhaps others, will not rest before the bring the Oracles into their grasp." Akhon smiled sadly as he continued, "After all, a full trained band of Oracles is something that the world hasn't seen for many years, and it is something that threatens to shake and challenge preexisting power structures, both here and in other places around the world. I'm quite certain that no order, the Elders or perhaps others, will allow that to happen without their control." Seeing them about to protest, Akhon put up a hand and closed his eyes as he said, "I know it does seem very far-fetched, considering I seriously doubt any of you have any true or innate desire for control, but power always fears power, and in the minds of many the only way to achieve and retain control is to bring others under your submission. Others will think these things when they deal with all of you." Akhon turned and looked at Taylor, Justin, Kitty, and Mignonne as he said, "Once you all begin working towards the fulfillment of your gifts, you will all become precious natural resources, and many will seek to control you, both separately and as a whole. You must guard against this, and as much as I will miss both my boys, I understand when destiny calls." At this Akhon stood and held out his arms as if trying to embrace Arkite, Sphinx, and everyone; "Go with grace, my dear *abna*, and may the Great Spirit lead, guide, and direct all of your pursuits!"

Mignonne, Kitty, Justin, Taylor, and Arkite all turned so that they were facing each other. After the turmoil of the confrontation, which coupled surprise from watching themselves and their abilities, and almost made each of them recoil from the others, unable to deal with the impossible that had just happened. For to Mignonne and Kitty it all seemed impossible, and they found themselves unable to sit back and believe that any of this had truly happened, it all seemed so farfetched and such a departure from their lives as they had always known them. The group might have stood there for an interminable amount of time, eyeing each other as if the others (or quite possibly *them*) were about to explode into action again and maybe bring the whole of the surrounding desert in on them! But because humans aren't able to maintain these times for long, whether they be regular or they have psycho-spiritual manifestations, it wasn't long after Akhon had made his grandiose pronouncement that Justin (who was still being regarded warily by the girls; new guy, after all), actually glanced towards Taylor, then Arkite and Akhon, and his shoulders started shaking as his stomach contorted. Justin bent over and looked like he was about to explode from suppressed emotion, whether from good or bad emotion even he wasn't quite certain. Laughter was trying to make its way out of him, it turns out, and eventually he lost all control of his self as a strangled sputtering sound made its way out of his mouth. Evidently figuring that it was too late now, Justin stood straight and threw his head back, heaving as wave after wave of laughter and mirth rocked his body, leaving him breathless and heaving before the fact that laughter is contagious was made evident. Nobody in the chamber at this point stood against this, and Kitty found herself torn between her astonishment at what had taken place and the stupid, care-free glee which was emitting from Justin. Relieved to have some-body break the spell of dolor that was emanating over the room, Mig-nonne joined in with the laughing much more quickly than the others, but starting with Sphinx and Akhon, eventually Taylor, Kitty, and fi-nally Arkite were overtaken, and the desert sun hung over the sand dunes and seemed to smile on the five Oracles as they laughed their way into the future that was their destiny.

Afterword

The morning dawned tentatively, covered with clouds and chilly air, as Taylor made his way into the living room, devoutly hoping that somebody, *anybody* had overcome their pride at the task and actually made coffee, tea, or any other hot beverage. Of course, that also required the hope that he wasn't the first one down, but he didn't think so. He wasn't actually sure if Arkite slept like a normal person. Upon entering, he exchanged a nod with Justin, who was often up almost as early as Arkite, and who, thanks be, was clutching a mug of American bliss in spite of their surroundings. Taylor was still trying to wake up as he grabbed a cup and flipped on the news, but a loud banging on the back door caused him to jump and turn his head in surprise. Justin and Taylor exchanged a look before Justin slowly and cautiously stood up off the couch and eased himself into the hallway. A still in pajamas Mignonne could be seen coming down the stairs; "Justin, what the hell? It's barely six o'clock in the morning, and even if it was later, why are you hitting something!?" Justin, as was often his way, gave Mignonne a scornful look before he turned back and kept walking to the doorway. In the dark, half-light of the morning, he approached and tried to see out of the glass over the door top but was thrown backwards as the door was flung open from the outside and Ishept and Omage burst into the hallway. His heart hammering in shock, Justin almost didn't recover in time to right himself and stand and block the small passageway. He desperately threw his arms wall to wall, seething and panting in fury as he faced these none too welcome intruders. Mignonne and Taylor came up behind him to investigate the commotion, and Omage smiled sardonically at this opposition. "Oh, my dear Oracles," he breathed out condescendingly, "I and Ishept are calling quite early this morning in order to convey news of unimaginable importance." Mignonne felt her heart immediately begin to race at this, and it was with eyes that were both worried and curious that she kept Omage's gaze. Justin and Taylor stared willfully at Omage, with Justin thinking that this had better be a really, *really* important talk.

CPSIA information can be obtained
at www.ICGtesting.com
Printed in the USA
BVHW041707210621
610126BV00010B/2115